### "Have I ever mentioned that you are absolutely gorgeous?"

Trevor raised his head from where he'd been conducting a thorough exploration of Jamie's chest. "Men aren't gorgeous," he said gruffly.

"That's what I'd always thought," Jamie said. Then she chuckled softly. "But I have to tell you, it always ticked me off that you were so much prettier than I was. Lucky for you, I'm getting over it."

"You're something else, you know that?" Trevor shook his head in exasperation. "Would you be quiet for a minute? I'm trying to seduce you here."

Jamie grinned, and then shivered as his hand accidentally touched a sensitive spot. "Uh, Trev? Maybe you haven't realized this, but I'm pretty well seduced already."

He sat up and brought his hands to her waist, easing her skirt down her hips and revealing her skimpy bikini panties. "I should have known that you wouldn't even take this seriously," he grumbled, as he dropped kisses along her thigh, her hip, before tossing aside her panties.

But Jamie was anything but amused when Trevor stood back and kicked off his pants, proving to her just how much he wanted her. Her mouth went dry as he returned to her and finally brought them flesh to flesh.

"Trust me, Trev," Jamie groaned in delight. "I'm taking this *very* seriously."

Dear Reader,

When I originally conceived the SOUTHERN
SCANDALS miniseries, I planned for it to be four
books—the McBride cousins, Savannah, Tara, Emily
and Emily's long-lost brother, Lucas. But it turned
out that Honoria, Georgia, wasn't so easy to leave.
The remaining McBrides—Tara's brothers, Trent and
Trevor—insisted on having stories of their own....

Unlike the rest of his rebellious family, Trevor McBride
had always taken pride in his respectability...until a
scandal involving his late wife brings him home to
Honoria in secret disgrace. His problems are compounded
when he comes face-to-face with a woman he has
never been able to forget—Jamie Flaherty, who's come
home to face her own demons. Trevor isn't sure he's
"wild" enough to capture Jamie's heart...but he's sure
willing to try. And he discovers a few surprises about
Jamie—and himself—along the way.

Coming next month, Trevor's brother, Trent, meets his
match in *Secretly Yours*. And be sure to watch for my
first single-title release, *Yesterday's Scandal*, on sale in
September. You'll meet a McBride no one in Honoria
has met before—including his own family!

I hope you enjoy visiting with THE WILD McBRIDES!

Gina Wilkins

## Books by Gina Wilkins

**HARLEQUIN TEMPTATION**
668—SEDUCING SAVANNAH*
676—TEMPTING TARA*
684—ENTICING EMILY*
710—THE REBEL'S RETURN*

*SOUTHERN SCANDALS

# Gina Wilkins
# SEDUCTIVELY YOURS

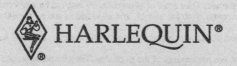

# HARLEQUIN®

TORONTO • NEW YORK • LONDON
AMSTERDAM • PARIS • SYDNEY • HAMBURG
STOCKHOLM • ATHENS • TOKYO • MILAN • MADRID
PRAGUE • WARSAW • BUDAPEST • AUCKLAND

For my agent of fifteen years,
Denise Marcil,
my partner and my friend.

ISBN 0-373-25892-5

SEDUCTIVELY YOURS

FOR GENERATIONS, scandal had haunted the McBrides
like an avenging spirit. At times, Trevor McBride felt
as if the sole purpose of his family's existence had
been to provide fodder for the avid gossips of Honoria, Georgia. Yet up until now, he had considered
himself immune to the curse.

A straight-A student in high school, town baseball
star, college scholarship winner and distinguished
graduate, he'd gone directly from law school to
Washington, D.C., where he'd quickly earned notice
as an up-and-coming young statesman. His marriage
to a woman from a distinguished and scandal-free
old Virginia family had produced two beautiful children, and had generally been regarded to be happy
and successful.

Trevor had managed to evade his family legacy for
thirty-one years. But he'd just discovered, to his cha-
grin, that scandal would not accept rejection from a
McBride. And when it finally made an appearance in
Trevor's life, it did so with a vengeance. He was finally learning to ignore the whispers, for the most
part, but he had never learned to accept them.

Out of the corner of his eye, he saw Martha Godwin
and Nellie Hankins watching him as he pushed a gro-
cery cart down the cereal aisle. Their mouths moved

rapidly and he had no doubt *he* was the subject of their conversation—even though, unlike the scandal-mongers in D.C., they didn't know the unpleasant details of his wife's death nearly a year earlier. No one in Honoria knew, and Trevor intended to keep it that way. "Come on, Sam," he said. "Stop dawdling."

His five-year-old son had stopped to examine a particularly enticing box. "Can we get this one, Daddy?"

Trevor glanced at it. Chocolate puffs with choco-late-flavored marshmallows. "Don't think that's a good choice, son. Let's stick with what we've got. Now, come on. Abbie's getting hungry."

"Me, too." Sam abandoned the sugar-laden cereal and hurried after his father and sister. "Can I have a Fun Meal? They're giving away race cars this week."

Looking at the shopping cart filled with nutritious food, Trevor almost sighed at his son's daily request for a dry burger and greasy fries accompanied by an inexpensive toy. He tried to give in to the request no more than a couple of times a month. "Not tonight, Sam."

From her seat in the shopping cart, fourteen-month-old Abbie babbled something incomprehen-sible. Trevor gave her a distracted smile and pushed the cart past the gossip mavens, hoping they would be content to talk about him without feeling the need to talk *to* him. Maybe if he pretended not to notice them...

"Trevor. Oh, Trevor, dear."

He would have cursed if his children hadn't been listening. Reluctantly realizing a conversation was inevitable, he stopped and turned, feeling Sam crowding close to him. He made no effort to smile, but he spoke cordially enough. "Good evening, Mrs. Godwin."

Nellie Hankins, he noticed, had bustled away. No Hankins would be seen associating with a McBride—the result of another old scandal.

Martha Godwin, blessed with all the tact of a tornado, moved to stand directly between him and the cash registers. "How have you been, Trevor? We haven't seen you around much lately."

"I've been busy, Mrs. Godwin."

Her expression changed to one he detested, but had seen far too often during the past year—cloying pity. "Poor dear. It must be so difficult for you trying to raise these two adorable children on your own."

Sam pressed his face more tightly into Trevor's leg. Sam hated having attention focused on him—especially this sort of attention. Abbie babbled and crammed her fist in her mouth, slobbering enthusiastically.

"Precious child," Martha crooned.

Abbie blew bubbles, making a sound that summed up the way Trevor was feeling. "Excuse me, Mrs. Godwin, the kids are hungry. Goodbye."

He moved the cart forward so that she was forced to move aside or risk losing a few toes. She left in a dignified huff when it became obvious that she would pry no interesting comments out of Trevor today.

"Guess you put that old battle-ax in her place." The supermarket checker spoke with a satisfaction that bespoke her experience of being on the wrong end of Martha's gossip.

Ignoring her, Trevor waited impatiently to escape the supermarket and get back to the blessed privacy of his own home.

ON THE FIRST DAY of her summer vacation, Jamie Flaherty sighed happily and wiggled her brightly painted toenails, letting the sun soak into her mostly bared skin. She wouldn't stay out long, she promised herself, thinking of all the damage excessive exposure could do to a woman's skin. But it felt so good to just sit and soak up rays for a few blissfully lazy moments.

In the end, it was vanity that forced her to move into the protective shade of a poolside awning. A few months away from her twenty-ninth birthday, she had no intention of risking premature wrinkles; she planned to fight aging as long as modern technology made it possible.

She slid a pair of sunglasses from the top of her head onto her nose and glanced around, taking stock of the others who were enjoying the neighborhood pool on this Monday afternoon in early June. There weren't many, since most people worked on weekdays—unless, like Jamie, they were fortunate enough to have summers off. Five or six children made use of the shallow end of the pool, some in inflated armbands, others showing off swim-class skills. Three women sat in chairs nearby, chatting as they kept watch over their kids.

A little boy of four or five sat on the edge of the

pool about halfway down, splashing his feet in the deeper water. His blond hair was dry, and he didn't look as though he'd been in the pool at all. He didn't seem unhappy or bored, Jamie decided. Just thoughtful. There was only one adult in the water, a young woman playing with a squealing toddler in a floating plastic seat. The little girl was blond, and reminded Jamie of the boy sitting on the side of the pool. Siblings?

And then her attention wandered again.

At the deeper end of the pool, near the diving board, half a dozen teenagers postured for each other, though most of the local teens hung out at the more popular new pool on the west side of town. A young lifeguard slouched in an elevated seat, his attention focused more on a couple of pretty teenage bodies than on his duties.

Stretching out in her shaded lounge chair, Jamie smiled as she remembered the long-ago days when she and other girls her age had worked so diligently—but so subtly, they had believed—to distract buff young lifeguards. Her smile deepened as she fondly recalled how often they had succeeded.

"I know that smile. It always means you're up to mischief," a familiar voice observed.

"Just remembering mischief." Jamie nodded toward the bikinied teenagers posing for the lifeguard's benefit.

Susan Schedler groaned as she lowered her very pregnant body into the chair next to Jamie's. "Oh, God. Was I ever that young and thin?"

"Hey, we were hot stuff." Jamie pulled her gaze

away from the girls to smile fondly at her longtime friend.

Susan glanced pointedly at Jamie's hot-pink bikini. "One of us still is."

"That's very nice. Thank you."

"Just stating facts." Susan lay back in her chair and rested a hand lightly on her bulging belly.

"How are you feeling today?"

Since Jamie had asked, Susan launched into a detailed analysis of her condition and how impatient she was to reach the end of it. Most of her attention on her friend's words, Jamie allowed her gaze to wander again. The teens had stepped up their flirting, she noticed. One of the girls had "accidentally" positioned herself so the lifeguard could look straight down her bikini top. With a frown, Jamie realized that he was taking full advantage of the silent offer.

While she had identified with the kids earlier, it perturbed her that the lifeguard was allowing his concentration to be drawn away from the pool. Jamie had worked as a lifeguard for three summers, and she knew the young man had been trained to resist distractions.

She glanced again at the shallow end, where children were still splashing and squealing. The young woman still played with the toddler in the floating seat, and the three women in the poolside chairs were heavily into a gossip session. Murmuring a response to something Susan said, Jamie turned her eyes to the spot where the little boy had been sitting. He'd moved, she noted. He'd probably given in to the lure of the cool water. She looked at the shallow end again, casually searching for his golden head among the other kids. She didn't see him. Was she simply overlooking him? Kids looked different wet, of course.

Something drew her eyes back to the spot where she'd last seen him. The water was just over eight feet deep there, she estimated. She knew there were kids below the age of six who swam like fish, but he'd looked so small and alone.

She glanced automatically toward the bottom of the pool.

A moment later, she was on her feet, her heart in her throat. She reached the side in two steps, slinging off her sunglasses before making a clean, shallow dive.

The boy was lying facedown on the bottom of the pool. Jamie scooped him into one arm and kicked forcefully toward the surface. By the time she reached the side of the pool, the others had just realized what was taking place. The lifeguard, his face pale, was there immediately to lift the little boy out of her arms.

Jamie heard someone scream, heard a couple of the younger children start to cry, heard the panicked, excited babbling of the teenagers, but her eyes were on the child as she boosted herself out of the pool and rushed to kneel beside him. Still flustered by being caught so unprepared, the lifeguard hesitated, and Jamie automatically took charge. The child had a pulse, thank God, but he didn't seem to be breathing. She rolled him onto his side, and lifted one arm above his head, hoping that would clear his lungs. She was prepared to do artificial respiration, but she was incredibly relieved when he began to cough and gag.

Steadying him, Jamie watched as liquid sputtered from his mouth. He'd taken some water into his lungs, she realized, relieved that someone had run to call an ambulance. He hadn't been underwater more than a couple of minutes, so there should be minimal danger of brain damage, but there was always a chance of complications from water in the lungs. Pneumonia, for one, she remembered. The child should definitely be checked out by trained medical personnel.

He was crying now, in choked, gulping sobs. Jamie drew him into her arms, murmuring reassurances. "You'll be fine, sweetie. Just fine."

"I didn't see him," the lifeguard muttered in a trembling voice. "I never even heard a splash."

"A child this small doesn't make much of a splash," Jamie answered, trying to speak gently despite her annoyance with him. She could tell he would pay for his negligence by painfully imagining what might have happened had she not been there.

"Oh, God, is Sam all right? His dad is going to kill me." The young woman who'd been playing with the toddler rushed to Jamie's side, the dripping little girl on her hip.

The boy—Sam—buried his face more tightly in her neck, whimpering and shivering. Instincts Jamie hadn't known she possessed kicked in, making her cradle the wet little body closer. Suddenly feeling smothered by the pressing crowd of gawkers, she looked at the lifeguard. "Maybe you could send everyone back to what they were doing?" she suggested in a low murmur.

He nodded, gathered his composure and stood, giving a short blast of his whistle. "Okay, everyone, back up and give the kid some room. You're making him nervous staring at him this way."

Even as the spectators slowly moved away, Jamie could hear a siren approaching in the distance. She looked up at the frantic woman with the little girl on her hip. The woman couldn't have been much more than twenty. Her face was pale, her eyes wide and horrified as she stared at the shivering boy. "Is he yours?" Jamie asked.

"I'm their nanny. Oh, ma'am, is Sam all right? I'll never forgive myself if—"

"He's fine," Jamie broke in quickly, patting the boy's back and speaking in a tone meant to calm both him and the overwrought nanny. "Sam's going to be just fine."

"He was sitting on the side," the nanny babbled. "He wouldn't come in the water, so I told him to stay put while I played with Abbie. I checked on him a couple of times and he was fine. Then I looked at Abbie again, and the next thing I knew, you were pulling him out of the pool. Sam, why did you go in the water? You know you can't swim."

"I slipped," the child murmured into Jamie's neck. "I was just going to stand up and I fell in the water."

"It's okay," Jamie said. "No one's blaming you, Sam." There was plenty of blame to spread around, she thought, but none of it was Sam's.

Two medics rushed into the fenced pool area.

Sam's arms had to be pried from around Jamie's neck. Apparently painfully shy of strangers, he refused to respond when the medics tried to talk to him, and he cried when they told him they were going to take him to be checked out.

"Go with me," he begged Jamie.

Startled by the request, she stroked his wet hair. "Your nanny and your little sister will go with you, Sam."

"He doesn't like me much," the young nanny said morosely. "I don't know why."

Jamie had a few guesses, but she kept them to herself. "You'll be fine, Sam," she assured the frightened little boy. "These people are very nice and they'll take good care of you."

"I'll call your dad and have him meet us at the hospital," his nanny promised. "You know he'll drop everything and be there in no time."

That seemed to reassure him. "My daddy will be there?"

"As soon as I call him." She seemed to have no doubt about it.

"Sam," little Abbie said from the nanny's hip, waving happily at her brother.

Sam allowed himself to be taken away, though he looked soulfully over his shoulder at Jamie—as though he was leaving his only friend behind, she thought with an odd feeling.

She scraped her fingers through her short, wet, red hair, pushing it away from her face as she watched them leave. The lifeguard turned sheepishly to Jamie. "I'm sure glad you were here, ma'am."

"Just keep your mind on your job from now on, okay?" Reaction had finally set in, leaving her weak-kneed and a bit shaky.

"I will," he said fervently, and dashed back to his post.

The teenagers had gathered again at the other side, the incident already forgotten since it didn't actually affect them. The three women who'd been sitting by the shallow end of the pool earlier were gathering their charges and their possessions, ready to leave as dinnertime approached. Susan, who had stayed back out of the way during the excitement, put her hand on Jamie's shoulder. "Are you okay?"

Jamie's smile felt lopsided. "I'm fine."

"That was amazing, Jamie. You moved so fast, my head is still spinning. If you hadn't been here..."

Jamie didn't even want to think about that. "I just happened to notice him. I guess old lifeguard habits die hard."

"At least *someone* around here benefited from rescue training." Susan looked darkly at the lifeguard, who sat now watching the almost-empty pool with intense vigilance. "With all the people at the pool today, word will get out. I'm sure he'll be reprimanded for what almost happened."

Jamie remembered the stricken look in the young man's eyes. "I think he learned his lesson."

Susan held out Jamie's sunglasses. "These are yours, I believe."

She took them and slid them onto her nose. "Thanks."

Making a production of wiping her forehead, Susan sighed gustily. "To think I came to the pool to relax for a few minutes. How could I have guessed it would be this exciting?"

Almost shuddering as she recalled the moment she'd spotted little Sam at the bottom of the pool—and knowing she would be haunted by that image for some time—Jamie murmured, "Personally, I could have done without the excitement."

Susan turned serious again. "What you did was incredible, Jamie. Maybe someone else would have spotted him in time to save him, but there's no guarantee. And by getting to him so quickly, you probably prevented him from having any lasting repercussions."

Jamie was becoming embarrassed by Susan's praise. "I'm just glad I was here to help," she said dismissively, matching her steps to her friend's as they walked together toward the exit.

"Not half as glad as Trevor McBride's going to be," Susan commented.

Jamie stumbled. *Trevor McBride?* She steadied herself quickly. "What does Trevor McBride have to do with anything?"

Susan's eyebrows rose. "Didn't you know? Sam is Trevor's son."

"No," Jamie murmured, turning her face to hide her expression. "I didn't know."

*Trevor's son.* The incident had just taken on a whole new significance for her.

Had things turned out the way she had once fantasized, *she* would have been the mother of Trevor McBride's children.

"YOU'RE SURE he's going to be okay? There's nothing else I should watch for?" Trevor couldn't seem to let go of his son, who had been clinging tightly to his neck for the past twenty minutes.

The doctor who had examined the boy smiled reassuringly. "Sam's going to be fine, Mr. McBride. He took in very little water and he was apparently conscious throughout the entire episode. According to your nanny, he was only underwater for a very short time. He was more terrified than anything. You should probably watch for emotional repercussions. Perhaps you should get him into swimming lessons soon to keep him from developing a permanent fear of water as a result of this."

"Thanks. I'll keep your advice in mind."

Just the mention of swimming lessons had made Sam hide his face again. He'd never liked water, and didn't trust strangers enough to take instructions easily from them—something Trevor was hoping they could change by the time he started kindergarten.

Becky Rhodes, the nanny Trevor had hired only a month earlier, was sitting in the waiting room with Abbie, who'd fallen asleep on her lap. She looked up anxiously when Trevor carried Sam out of the examining room. "Is he okay?"

"He's fine," Trevor answered shortly, resisting an impulse to add, *No thanks to you.*

Becky sagged in relief. "I'm so glad. I'm really sorry about this, Mr. McBride. I was busy with Abbie and he just fell in. I never saw him."

Trevor's arms tightened instinctively around his son. "Thank God the lifeguard saw him."

Becky snorted. "The lifeguard had nothing to do with it. He was too busy flirting with a bunch of girls. If that woman hadn't noticed Sam in the pool..."

Trevor had rushed straight into the examining room upon his arrival at the hospital. He hadn't yet heard the details of his son's rescue. "What woman?"

"The new drama teacher at the high school. You know, the one with the really red hair and lots of earrings and cool clothes? Ms. Flaherty. I think her first name is Jamie."

"Jamie Flaherty," Trevor murmured, his mind filling with almost fifteen-year-old memories of a young woman who had tempted him to be wild and reckless for the first time in his life. "Jamie Flaherty saved my son?"

Eyeing him a bit warily, Becky nodded. "Yes."

Masking his feelings, Trevor motioned toward the exit. "I'll drive you home. Can you carry Abbie?"

"Of course." Becky shifted the sleeping baby to her shoulder.

Trevor scooped up the diaper bag and followed her out of the hospital, grimly aware that there were several things he had to take care of that evening—and none of them were going to be easy. Finding Jamie Flaherty to thank her for rescuing his son was one of the most awkward, but necessary, chores he faced.

The last time he had talked to Jamie, he'd rather bluntly told her that his future plans did not include her. Holding his son tightly in his arms, he was aware of a mixed sense of gratitude and dismay that she had reappeared in his life at this particular time.

# 2

IT WAS NEARLY EIGHT that evening when Trevor rang Jamie's doorbell. She lived only a few blocks away, though her little bungalow was considerably smaller than the two-story, four-bedroom house he'd purchased after moving back to Honoria ten months ago.

He had never expected to find himself on her doorstep.

He rang the bell again. He could hear music playing inside. Loud, pulsing rock music. No wonder she couldn't hear the bell. Maybe he should just forget about this, he thought, glancing toward his car. But she had saved his son's life. The very least he owed her was a thank-you. He pressed the bell again. The music abruptly stopped.

"All right," a woman's voice called. "I'm coming. Keep your pants on, okay?"

She opened the door. After only a moment's pause, she cocked her head and planted a hand on her slender hip. "Why, Trevor McBride. Fancy finding you here."

The last time Trevor had last seen Jamie, she had been a sophomore in high school, he'd been a senior. Despite her instant recognition, he knew he'd changed a great deal since then. With the exception of her hair color, he couldn't see that Jamie had changed much at all. The years had been extremely kind to her.

He took a moment to study her. Looking as though she had just run her hand through it, her dark red hair stood in damp spikes around her face, which was flushed and beaded with perspiration. She wore a towel around her neck, a turquoise T-shirt, black shorts, baggy socks and expensive-looking athletic shoes. Several stud earrings decorated each of her ears, but he didn't see any other jewelry. If she had worn any makeup earlier, it was gone now.

The grubby look had never particularly appealed to him. But on Jamie, it was most definitely appealing. He had always found himself drawn to her, even when he'd made every effort to resist the attraction.

That was something else that hadn't changed, apparently.

He lifted his gaze to her face, seeing himself reflected in her vividly green eyes. "Did I interrupt something?"

"Tae-Bo." She wiped her face with one corner of the towel. "Wanna join me for a quick punch-and-kick?"

"No, thank you," he answered politely.

She grinned. "The last time we talked, I think I asked if you wanted to duck behind the gym for a little kiss-and-grope," she mused. "And I'm pretty sure you took me up on it."

He cleared his throat, refusing to be drawn into his youthful indiscretions. He definitely remembered when he had first kissed her behind the gym. And he remembered just as clearly telling her it couldn't happen again. Even though it had on an occasion or two. "The reason I'm here..."

She laughed...exactly the same way she'd laughed at him almost fifteen years ago. And it made him feel as awkward and self-conscious now as it had then. How could she still do that to him? "I know why you're here," she said. "And it has nothing to do with a stroll down memory lane."

"No. I wanted to..."

She moved out of the doorway. "Come in, Trev. I need a drink."

No one else had ever called him Trev. He wouldn't have let anyone else get away with it. Somehow, it had always sounded sort of natural coming from Jamie. "I can't stay long," he said, glancing at his watch. "My mom's sitting with the kids and—"

"We'll just have a quick drink," she said over her shoulder.

He could either follow her or be left standing alone on her porch. With a rather wistful glance back at his car, he stepped through the doorway and closed the door behind him.

It was no surprise to discover that Jamie's decorating was as vivid and unconventional as she was. An almost dizzying array of fabrics and colors clashed and competed with a number of objects Jamie had collected. His gaze slid from a six-inch plastic Statue of Liberty to a porcelain figurine of Marilyn Monroe, then paused for a moment on one of the dozens of framed photographs in the room. This one showed Jamie snuggled up to a man who looked suspiciously like a famous television comedian. Next to it was a shot of Jamie mugging with an Academy Award–winning actress.

There were others, but he didn't take time to study them all. Nor would he allow himself to be impressed. After all, Jamie's New York acting career had lasted less than ten years, and now she was teaching drama at the local high school. Like him, Jamie had ended up right back where she had started.

He wondered if her return had been any happier than his own.

Without bothering to ask if he wanted anything, Jamie poured bottled water over two glasses of ice and pressed one into his hand. She drank half her own without pausing for air, then set the glass on the counter, her full, unpainted lips glistening with drops of moisture. "Before you launch into the speech I'm sure you've carefully prepared, I just want to say that there's really no need. I happened to be close by when your son fell into the pool this afternoon and I jumped in to pull him out. Anyone else would have done the same thing."

"But no one else did," he replied. "You saved Sam's life, Jamie. There's no way for me to adequately express my gratitude."

"Let's just stick with 'thank you' and 'you're welcome,' shall we?"

His lips twitched, though he was trying not to smile. This was too important. "Thank you."

She nodded briskly. "You're welcome."

"It isn't enough, you know. Not for what you did."

She shrugged. "I'm just glad I was there."

"So am I," he agreed, his tone heartfelt.

She picked up her glass. "Let's take these into the living room."

Once again, he had to follow or be left behind. He took a sip of his water, then left the full glass on the counter as he trailed her into the other room. "Jamie..."

She kicked off her shoes and curled up on her jewel-tone striped couch, waving him into a nearby chair. "Your kids are adorable, Trevor."

"Thank you." He wasn't sure what else to say. He had expressed his gratitude—at least, as much as she had allowed him to—which was all he'd intended to do. He hadn't planned on an extended visit. After all, despite a couple of memorable past encounters, he and Jamie Flaherty were basically strangers.

"How old are they?"

"Sam turned five last month. Abbie's fourteen months."

"I heard that your wife died last year. I'm sorry."

He had no intention of talking about his late wife. He merely nodded in response to her expression of sympathy.

"Are you a good father?"

She asked the question completely seriously, as if he should be able to easily reply with a simple yes or no. Even when they were kids, he'd never known quite how to respond to many of the things Jamie said. "I do my best."

"Your nanny—"

"I fired her this evening."

Jamie blinked. "You *fired* her?"

"She almost let my son drown. She told me herself

that she never saw him go in the water. She knew he couldn't swim."

"She was playing with Abbie. She seemed very fond of her."

"Yes, she was good with Abbie," he conceded. "But she didn't bond well with Sam. Because she couldn't communicate well with him, she tended to ignore him. I have two kids. I need someone who will look after both of them while I'm working."

Jamie studied his face a moment. "You always were a bit intolerant of other people's failings."

"When it comes to my children's safety, I will always demand perfection," he answered flatly, oddly stung by her criticism.

"Of course."

He couldn't quite read her expression now. Satisfied that he'd made his point, he added, "Tomorrow, I'll make sure that sorry excuse for a lifeguard loses his job, as well."

"I hope you don't do that. He's young. The pool's only been open for a couple of weeks. He was completely shaken by what almost happened today. I'm sure he'll be more vigilant from now on."

"Not at the pool where my children swim, he won't."

Jamie's eyes narrowed. "Funny," she said, her voice soft. "I remembered you being stuffy and arrogant, but I never thought of you as a complete jerk."

"Jamie, he almost let my son drown!"

"He made a mistake. A huge one, I'll admit, but I think he deserves a second chance. Do you expect me to believe that you have never in your life made a mistake, Trevor McBride?"

"No." His voice was grim. "I don't expect you to believe that."

"Give the boy another chance. Have him reprimanded, if you like—or do it yourself—but don't make him lose his job."

Even when they'd been young, even when Trevor had known Jamie would only bring him trouble, she'd always been able to sway him. He sighed. "All right. I won't have him fired. But I hope you're right that he'll do a better job in the future. Lives literally depend on it."

"I know. And I wouldn't risk them recklessly," she assured him.

"I'll take your word for it." He watched as she shifted on the couch, folding her long, bare legs into a more comfortable position. Her baggy shorts gapped at the tops of her legs, revealing intriguing glimpses of smooth thighs. His reaction to those glimpses made him scowl and abruptly raise his gaze to her face again. "I heard you'd moved back here," he said. "I have to admit I was surprised."

"I came back in March," she acknowledged. "My aunt, who still teaches at the elementary school, called me about the opening for a drama teacher at the high school for the remainder of the second semester. The former teacher hadn't planned to leave for a couple of years, but when her husband was diagnosed with cancer, she retired to take care of him. They needed someone on very short notice, and I just happened to be available."

"I didn't even know you had teaching credentials."

"My college degree was in secondary education with a theater minor. I've always believed in having a back-up plan, and teaching was mine. I worked as a sub in New York schools between acting gigs. This job's a piece of cake compared to that experience."

"I can imagine. So, are you staying on now that the school year's finished, or are you headed back to Broadway?"

"I spent much more time off-Broadway and off-*off*-Broadway," she corrected him with a wrinkle of her short nose. "I was ready for a change. I've signed on for another year at Honoria High. The kids want to put on a production of *Grease* in the spring, and I promised to help them."

"Sounds like a big job."

"It should take most of the school year to put it to-gether. We're going to do a smaller production in De-cember—*A Christmas Carol,* maybe, or *The Best Christ-mas Pageant Ever.* I'll also be teaching speech classes."

"So you're giving up acting?"

"I didn't say that. I'm just taking a break for a cou-ple of years."

Trevor knew what a two-year "break" could do to an acting career—especially for a woman nearing thirty. There was more to Jamie's story than she had told him—not that it was any of his business, of course. But he wondered how long she would be con-tent to live in Honoria after her years in New York.

He wondered how many people were speculating about him in much the same way.

Glancing again at his watch, he stood. "I have to

get back to the kids. Thanks again, Jamie. If you ever need anything...I owe you one."

Her mouth tilted into a funny smile. "I'll keep that in mind." She pushed herself slowly off the couch and walked him to the door. "It's good to see you again, Trev."

"It's good to see you, too." Which was, he decided, the truth in a strange sort of way. "Good night, Jamie."

Her arm brushed his when she reached unexpectedly around him to open the door. His reaction to the casual touch seemed out of proportion—which only illustrated how stressful his day had been, he mused. It had left him completely rattled. He made his exit while he could still do so with something approaching dignity.

JAMIE WAITED until Trevor had closed the door behind him before she sagged bonelessly onto the couch. Oh, wow, she thought dazedly. The guy had been gorgeous in high school. He was even more so now that he had a few years of maturity on him.

He still seemed as skittish and elusive with her as he had ever been. And he still looked at her in a way that made her heart pound in her throat. It gave her some comfort that she had managed to hide her reactions to him.

This time, she told herself, she would not let Trevor break her heart. If anything happened between them now—and she still wasn't ruling that out—it would be on *her* terms.

AS WITH MOST small Southern towns, shopping at the local discount superstore in Honoria was a major social event. Sooner or later, everyone ended up there. It was almost impossible to stop in even to grab a couple of items without running into someone you knew. There were several women who wouldn't dare go shopping for toilet paper without doing their hair and makeup.

Dressed in a striped tank top, khaki shorts and heavy leather sandals, Jamie ran a hand through her short hair and applied a light coating of lip gloss, the full extent of her primping before she entered the store Friday afternoon. She bumped into three people before she could even claim a shopping cart. All of them wanted to talk about what had happened at the swimming pool earlier in the week.

She was exasperated, but not particularly surprised, to learn that the incident had become rather exaggerated in the frequent retelling—particularly her part in it.

"Risking your own life to save that boy," silver-haired Mildred Scott said in breathless admiration. "You should be given some sort of award for heroism, Jamie."

Gripping the rickety cart she'd managed to snag, Jamie answered with strained patience. "My life was never at risk, Mrs. Scott. The water wasn't all that deep. All I did was lift the boy out."

Clearly preferring the more interesting version she'd heard, Mrs. Scott smiled knowingly and patted Jamie's arm. "You're being modest. That's very becoming of you, but I still think I'll ask Chief Davenport about that award. Or maybe the mayor."

"Mrs. Scott, I would really rather you didn't—"

Without waiting to be dissuaded, the older woman bustled away, as if to act while the idea was still fresh. Jamie sighed, shook her head in resignation and pushed her cart toward the health-and-beauty aids section of the store. A trio of teenagers emerged from the cosmetics aisle, their hands filled with rainbow-colored nail polishes, eye shadows and lip glosses. "Hi, Ms. Flaherty," they chimed in unison, instantly adopting the tone every kid seems to use around a schoolteacher.

Though she knew she didn't particularly look like a teacher at the moment, Jamie found herself automatically answering in her own "schoolmarm" voice. "Hello, girls. Enjoying your vacation so far?"

They all nodded eagerly, then hurried away, giggling and whispering. Feeling suddenly years older, Jamie tossed a box of facial tissues into her cart. Funny how age was relative, she mused as she moved toward the toothpaste section. To old Mrs. Scott, Jamie was still just a girl. But to the teenagers, her twenty-nine years must seem almost ancient.

Discount philosophy, she thought with a wry smile. How appropriate for her current surroundings. She added dental floss to her cart and headed for cleaning supplies.

The store was a noisy place. Frequent announcements sounded over the intercom, dozens of conversations swirled around her, mothers scolded whining children and several babies cried in shrill stereo. Jamie often enjoyed spending time just people-watching in places like this, but today she had quite a few other things she wanted to get done. She grabbed a spray bottle of glass cleaner from a shelf and tossed it on top of her other selections.

Two more items on her list, and she could escape.

A sudden tug at the hem of her shorts made her glance downward. She raised her eyebrows in surprise when she recognized the little blond boy gazing somberly up at her. "Well, hello, Sam."

"Hello," he replied without returning her smile. He kept his big blue eyes trained unwaveringly on her face.

"Are you here with your dad?" Jamie looked around for Trevor before turning her gaze back to Sam.

The boy shook his head. "I'm with Grandma."

"Where is she?"

"Over there." Sam pointed vaguely to one side.

"Does she know where you are?"

The boy shrugged, obviously unconcerned.

Funny child, Jamie thought, studying his serious little face. She assumed he laughed occasionally, but she had yet to hear it. He gazed up at her as if waiting for her to do or say something interesting, making her feel oddly self-conscious. "Um...so how are you, Sam?"

"Good," he answered, then fell silent again, still looking expectantly up at her.

She was thinking about bursting into a song-and-tap-dance number—just to keep from disappointing him—when Bobbie McBride's familiar voice came from behind her. "There you are, Sam! Why did you run off from me like... Oh, hello, Jamie."

Feeling much the way the teenagers who'd greeted her earlier had probably felt, Jamie responded politely to her former teacher. "Hello, Mrs. McBride."

Bobbie shook a finger at her. "I've told you to call me Bobbie. We're colleagues now. And I still owe you a big debt of gratitude for rescuing my grandson."

Since Bobbie had already telephoned Jamie to express her thanks, Jamie saw no need to go over it all again now. To change the subject, she smiled at the rosy-cheeked toddler in the seat of Bobbie's shopping cart. "Hi, Abbie. How are *you* today?"

"Moo," the tot replied clearly.

"We've been playing the animal-sounds game," Bobbie explained. "Abbie just told you what a cow says."

"Of course she did. That's very good, Abbie."

The little girl laughed and clapped her hands. Her more serious-natured brother tugged again at Jamie's shorts. "I got a new book," he said when he had her attention.

"Did you? What is it?"

Sam reached into his grandmother's cart. "This one."

"Berenstein Bears." Jamie nodded approval. "I've always enjoyed their stories. This looks like a good one."

"It's about Brother Bear and Sister Bear spending the night at their grandmother's house," Sam volunteered.

"Yes, I see. I'm sure you'll like it." She gave the book back to him. "Do you like to read, Sam?"

Bobbie, who wasn't known to be quiet for long, answered for her grandson. "Sam's always got a book in his hands—just like his daddy when *he* was a boy."

"All that reading certainly paid off for Trevor," she murmured. Jamie had once considered Trevor McBride the smartest boy at Honoria High. She'd also thought him the most attractive guy in Honoria. Remembering the way he'd looked the other night, with his neatly brushed dark blond hair, his serious blue eyes, his clean-shaven, strongly chiseled chin and cheekbones, she reminded herself that she hadn't changed her opinion about either of those things.

Bobbie abruptly changed the subject. "I'd like to have you to dinner. Our way of thanking you again for coming to Sam's rescue."

"That's very kind of you, but it isn't—"

"Are you free tomorrow evening? Seven o'clock?"

"Well, I—"

"Good. We'll look forward to seeing you then. Come along, Sam. We have to be going."

Sam was still gazing up at Jamie. "You're coming to dinner at Grandma's house?"

Jamie couldn't help wondering if anyone had ever successfully turned Bobbie down. "It seems that I am."

"Will you sit by me?"

"I would be delighted," she assured him.

Bobbie looked from her grandson to Jamie. "He certainly seems taken with you. He's usually shy with strangers."

"Sam and I are pals, aren't we, Sammy?"

He nodded and Jamie was pleased to see a shy smile playing at the corners of his mouth. Maybe she would even hear him laugh before the dinner party ended.

"Moo!" Abbie shouted gleefully, unwilling to be ignored for long.

Pushing the cart, Bobbie instructed Sam to follow her to the checkouts. He did, but he looked over his shoulder at Jamie until he was out of sight.

"Odd child," she murmured, shaking her head in bemusement. She supposed he came by it honestly. The McBrides were a notoriously offbeat family, though Bobbie and her husband Caleb seemed to be the least scandal-prone of the bunch.

EXPECTING BOBBIE TO ANSWER her doorbell the next evening, Jamie was caught momentarily off guard when Trevor opened the door, instead. She recovered quickly, regarding him with a faint smile she knew he would have trouble interpreting. "Hello, handsome."

She had always enjoyed flustering him, which probably explained why she tried to do so as often as possible. She figured it was as good a way as any to keep him from realizing how often he flustered *her*.

She had suffered such a huge crush on him when she'd been a teenager, a crush she'd hoped at times that he shared. She had made no secret of her attraction to him, and she'd done everything possible to get his attention. It had shattered her secret daydreams when he had told her on the night before his graduation that he wouldn't be seeing her anymore. He'd said they were too different—in age, in goals, in everything—and that there was no reason for them to pursue anything that couldn't go anywhere. He had graduated and gone off to the East Coast for college and law school, and then had settled in Washington, D.C., with a wife from a suitably aristocratic Virginia family.

Even *she* didn't know quite how she felt about him now, though her stomach still fluttered when he looked at her in that serious, searching way of his. Much the same way his son looked at her, she thought suddenly, realizing now why she'd reacted so strongly to young Sam.

A lot of things had changed since the last time she and Trevor had been together. The three-year age difference no longer mattered, and the very different career paths they had chosen to pursue had somehow led them back to the same place. She was becoming increasingly curious to find out what else had changed since he had so awkwardly let her down before.

Trevor chose to acknowledge her teasing greeting with a rather formal, "Good evening, Jamie. Please come in. Mother's in the kitchen putting finishing touches to dinner, but she'll be out soon."

She sauntered past him, giving an extra little flip to the vented skirt of her short, sleeveless sheath dress—just in case he was looking at her legs. She could hear several voices coming from the living room, and she turned to Trevor to stall for a moment before joining the others. "It was nice of your mother to invite me to dinner."

"Are you kidding? You're the family hero. Mom would have liked to have a parade in your honor, but she settled for a dinner party."

Jamie wrinkled her nose. "I tried to tell her it wasn't necessary to make such a big deal of this. I really didn't do anything all that spectacular."

"You saved my son," he said gently. "If Mom had insisted on a parade, I'd have gladly helped her plan it."

Had she been prone to blushing, she would have been beet red. Instead, she reverted to dry humor. "But would you lead the band? You'd look really cute wearing one of those tall hats and holding a baton."

He gave her a look. "As grateful as I am to you, there are limits."

She laughed, pleased that she'd provoked him into acting more natural. She really didn't want to spend the entire evening being treated like some sort of movie heroine—especially by Trevor.

She would just have to do her best to make him look at her in a different light, she mused.

# 3

CALEB MCBRIDE WAS the first to greet Jamie when Trevor escorted her into the living room. She smiled when he approached with a look of warm welcome on his pleasant face. Aware that there were other adults and several children in the room, she concentrated solely on her host for the moment.

Probably in his early sixties, Caleb had perfected the image of small-town Southern lawyer—genial, personable, courteous, but tough when he needed to be. Though she didn't know him very well, Jamie had always liked him, even as she suspected that he was as consummate an actor as any she'd met on stage. Perhaps it was purely circumstance, but Caleb couldn't have played his role in Honoria more perfectly if he'd followed a detailed script.

"It's good to see you, Jamie," he said, taking her hand in both of his. "After what you did, you will always be an honored guest in our home."

She hoped she wouldn't have to spend the entire evening trying to respond to comments like that. Deciding distraction was her best defense, she gave him a cheeky smile and said, "It's always good to see you, too, Mr. McBride. I swear, you get better-looking every time I see you. If you weren't married..."

He chuckled, obviously flattered. "If I weren't married, I would still be twice your age."

Someone tugged on her skirt. Jamie looked down.

"*I'm* not married," Sam assured her, gazing seriously up at her.

Everyone in the room laughed, except Jamie, who didn't want to hurt the boy's feelings—and Trevor, she noted peripherally. "Still playing the field, are you, Sam? That's understandable from a handsome young guy like you."

Though he didn't appear to quite understand Jamie's comment, Sam seemed satisfied to have momentarily claimed her attention. He stood close to her side when she turned to greet the others. She wasn't particularly surprised to see the police chief, Wade Davenport, and his wife, Emily. Emily was Caleb's niece, and had been a year behind Jamie in school. She had been the only McBride of her generation who had stayed and settled in Honoria instead of moving on in search of greener pastures. Trevor, of course, was the only one who had returned after moving away—for reasons Jamie couldn't help being curious about.

"How are you, Emily?" she asked.

Holding a baby no more than a few months old in her arms, the pretty, blue-eyed blonde beamed with visible contentment. "I'm fine, thank you, Jamie. You know my husband, Wade, of course?"

Jamie glanced at the solidly built, ruggedly attractive, thirty-something cop. "Hello, Chief. Caught any dangerous criminals lately?"

He gave her a lazy smile. "Not since I stopped you for speeding last week."

Hearing what might have been a faint sigh from Trevor, Jamie pouted for effect. "I was only going five miles over the speed limit."

"You were doing sixty in a forty-five zone and you know it," Wade retorted. "I let you off easy by only citing you for five-miles-over. Next time, I won't be so generous."

"Wade, Jamie just saved my grandson's life," Caleb chided. "Is it really necessary to threaten her this evening?"

"It wasn't a threat—just a warning."

Jamie smiled and stuck out her hand to him. "Warning heeded. I'll watch my speed from now on. And no hard feelings, Chief."

"Of course not." Wade shook her hand, then waved toward the red-haired lad sitting on the couch and playing a handheld electronic game. "This is my son, Clay. Boy, remember your manners, will you? Come shake hands with Ms. Flaherty."

Clay Davenport, whom Jamie judged to be around eleven, somewhat reluctantly set the game aside and rose. "Hello, Ms. Flaherty," he said, gravely shaking Jamie's hand.

"It's very nice to meet you, Clay."

"Ms. Flaherty's aunt was your fourth-grade teacher," Wade informed his son.

Jamie's smile deepened. "I think my aunt Ellen has taught every fourth-grader in Honoria for the past couple of generations."

Clay shook his head. "My friend Pete had Mrs. Simmons."

"She didn't mean it literally, Clay," Emily murmured, laying an affectionate hand on her stepson's shoulder while cradling her infant daughter in her other arm. "How is your aunt, Jamie?"

"I talked to her yesterday. You know she and Uncle Bill are spending the summer in North Carolina? They love it there."

"I'm happy to hear it. I understand she's retiring after this coming school year."

"Yes, they're thinking about relocating permanently to a condo in North Carolina."

"They'll be missed here."

Jamie was admiring baby Claire when Bobbie bustled into the room, immediately taking over with her brusque, authoritative manner. "Hello, Jamie. Glad you could make it. Dinner's about ready. All I have to do is set everything out. Give me five minutes. Trevor, I think I heard Abbie fussing."

Trevor nodded and moved toward the doorway. "I was just about to go check on her."

"I'll help you get dinner on the table, Aunt Bobbie," Emily offered, handing the baby to her husband.

Jamie stepped forward. "Is there anything I can do?"

Bobbie shook her head. "Thank you, dear, but you're our guest this evening. Visit with the men for a few minutes and we'll call everyone when it's time to eat."

Jamie was left in the living room with Caleb, Sam,

Wade, Clay and baby Claire. Sam still stood beside her, staring up at her in a way that reminded her of Eddie, the funny little terrier on the TV series *Frasier*. She was almost tempted to pat his head.

Caleb waved a hand toward the sofa. "Make yourself comfortable, Jamie. Can I get you anything to drink before dinner?"

"No, thank you." She settled on one end of the comfortably overstuffed couch. Sam scrambled onto the cushion beside her. Caleb sank into a worn-looking recliner that was obviously "his" chair, while Wade chose a wooden rocking chair for himself and his daughter. Clay sat cross-legged on the floor, his attention fully reclaimed by his electronic game.

Never one to savor silence, Jamie spoke up. "How are Tara and Trent, Mr. McBride? It's been ages since I've seen either of them."

Caleb seemed pleased that she'd asked about his other two offspring. "Tara and a partner have a small law practice in Atlanta. Tara's married to an unorthodox private investigator—Blake Fox—and they're expecting their first child soon."

Though Tara had been a few years ahead of her in school and they hadn't known each other well, Jamie wasn't surprised to hear that Tara was a successful attorney. She'd been an overachiever—just like her brother, Jamie thought as Trevor came back into the room carrying little Abbie. He sat on the opposite end of the couch, on the other side of Sam, balancing the toddler on his knee.

"Trent," Caleb continued, as if there had been no interruption, "graduated from the air force academy.

He's training to be a fighter pilot, stationed in California right now, but he's hoping for a transfer to Aviano, Italy, soon."

"I doubt that his mother likes that."

Caleb chuckled. "You've got that right. She complains frequently that all her children moved away from Honoria as soon as they graduated high school. She's delighted, of course, that Trevor has come home to us so she can see the grandkids as often as she likes."

Jamie turned to watch Trevor as he smoothed Abbie's nap-rumpled hair. The ease of his movements spoke of experience, and made her see him more clearly as a single father, solely responsible for two very young and very vulnerable children. It was up to him, she mused, to make sure that they were fed, bathed and clothed, to take them to the doctor and the dentist, to tuck them into bed, dry their tears and soothe their fears. Having never been accountable for anyone but herself—not even a pet—Jamie could hardly imagine such awesome responsibility.

She wondered again about the children's mother, who had died so tragically young. Trevor's wife. Was he still in mourning for her? Had he returned to Honoria for his mother's help with his children, or to escape the painful memories of his wife and the home they had shared in Washington? Maybe a little of both?

When she found herself wondering if he would ever fall in love again, she abruptly redirected her train of thought.

She turned to Wade. "I heard, of course, that Emily's brother Lucas reappeared a couple of years ago. The town gossips must have had a field day."

Wade nodded. "He came back for Christmas and stayed to attend our wedding on New Year's Eve, eighteen months ago. And, yeah, the gossips nearly wore out their tongues when he showed up out of the blue after being gone fifteen years. More than half the town believed he'd murdered Roger Jennings before he left, and they weren't too happy to hear he'd come back."

"From what I've heard, he's back in the town's good graces now that everyone knows it was Roger's uncle who was the real murderer. I could hardly believe that. Sam Jennings was my dentist when I was a kid! Who could have imagined then that he'd already killed twice and would kill again?"

"Lucas's innocence certainly swayed public opinion in his favor," Trevor commented dryly. "But not as much, perhaps, as the fact that he made himself a fortune in the California computer industry while he was away. The snobs were much more gracious to the rich businessman than they had been to the rebel he'd been before he left town."

"That I believe," Jamie murmured, thinking of times in the past when she had been shunned because of her own less-than-ideal family background. Being the only daughter of two alcoholics whose marital battles had been well know in the community, Jamie knew what it was like to grow up outside the tight social cliques in this town. "I'm glad Lucas has done well for himself. I understand he and Rachel Jennings were married and live in California."

"They seem very happy," Caleb agreed. "Lucas needed someone like Rachel to calm him down. He was always so hotheaded and volatile, and she's so calm and restrained—they offset each other very well. They announced just last week that they're expecting a baby. It'll be interesting to see what kind of father Lucas makes."

"Your family is growing rapidly," Jamie commented.

Caleb nodded in visible satisfaction. As the only surviving member of his generation, he must be pleased that the McBride name would carry on, Jamie decided.

"Uncle Lucas designed this game," young Clay remarked, proving that he'd been monitoring the adults' conversation while seemingly engrossed in his toy. "It's called a Rebelcom and it's way cool."

"You'll have to show it to me after dinner," Jamie suggested. "I have a weakness for cool electronics."

Clay nodded and pushed another game button, returning to his play.

"I got one, too," Sam piped up. "For my birthday. You can see mine, if you come to my house."

Jamie smiled down at her young admirer. "Maybe I'll do that sometime."

She didn't look at Trevor as she spoke, though she wondered how he felt about his son inviting her to their house.

"So now I've asked about all the McBride cousins except Savannah," she commented, turning back to Caleb. "I know from the grapevine that she married the writer Christopher Pace and they divide their time between L.A. and Georgia. I assume she's doing well?"

Caleb nodded at the mention of his late brother's only daughter. "Savannah's fine. Seems happy as a clam. Her husband is a decent guy, even if he does hang out some with those Hollywood types."

Smiling, Jamie asked, "And her twins?"

"Teenagers now. Good kids, both of them, and they're crazy about Kit. He legally adopted them. I sort of hated to see them give up the McBride name, but it seems to have made them feel more like a family, so I guess they made the right decision."

Jamie hadn't forgotten the big scandal when Savannah McBride, head cheerleader, homecoming queen, beauty pageant winner and pampered princess, had become pregnant with twins when she was sixteen. Jamie had been only ten or eleven at the time, but everyone in Honoria had known about Savannah's predicament and the controversy that had ensued when she'd named Vince Hankins as the father—an accusation the high-school jock had cravenly denied. Jamie was glad Savannah and her children had turned out all right.

The McBrides had been providing fodder for the town gossips for years, she mused. It had been something that had made her feel a kinship with them, since she'd been the subject of some avid gossip herself during her admittedly reckless teen years.

"You haven't mentioned *your* family yet this evening," Caleb said, politely directing the conversations away from his own clan. "How is your mother?"

"She's fine." Jamie knew her tone had become

stilted, but it always did when she talked of her mother. "She's living in Birmingham now, close to her sister."

"And your father?"

She felt her neck muscles tighten even more when she replied. "Last I heard, he was living in Montana. We don't really stay in touch."

"I see."

There was a brief, awkward silence, which seemed to hold for several tense moments. Then Abbie laughed and babbled something, baby Claire fussed and Bobbie came into the room to announce that dinner was served. Relieved to have the attention diverted from herself, Jamie lifted her chin, pasted on a bright smile and rose to join the others as they moved toward the dining room.

THE MAIN COURSE was well under way by the time Trevor reached the conclusion that his son was seriously smitten. Sam had hardly taken his eyes off Jamie since she'd arrived. Unfortunately, Trevor was having a similar problem.

He knew what *he* saw in Jamie—the same things he'd noticed even back in high school. He couldn't imagine any normal male being entirely immune to Jamie Flaherty's less-than-subtle sexuality. But he wondered what it was about her that held his boy so enthralled. Her bright red hair—which, he recalled, had been a medium brown when he'd known her before? Her easy laugh and quick, expressive movements? The fact that she had saved Sam's life?

Jamie couldn't have been more opposite—outwardly, at least—to Trevor's late wife, Melanie. Melanie had been quiet, dignified, so prim and neatly groomed as to be almost porcelain perfect. She'd had a sense of humor, but it had been understated, restrained. If someone had put them side by side, one might have compared Jamie to the sun—bright, conspicuous, hot—and Melanie to the moon—pale, quiet, cool. Like the moon, Melanie had kept her dark side hidden, even from her husband.

Abbie interrupted his uncharacteristic daydreaming by banging her spoon on the tray of her high chair. She squealed in delight at the ensuing clang and did it again. Trevor reached over to catch her hand. "No, Abbie. Eat," he said, redirecting her attention to the bite-size pieces of food on the unbreakable plate in front of her.

Gazing at him with blue eyes that were exactly like her mother's, Abbie gave him a slobbery grin. "Daddy," she said.

His throat contracted, a now-familiar mixture of love and heartache he often felt when he looked at his tiny daughter. "Eat your dinner, Abbie," he repeated a bit gruffly, holding a slice of banana to her rosy lips.

Once she was busy with her food again, he turned back to his own plate. His gaze collided abruptly with Jamie's across the table, and he resisted the impulse to squirm in his seat. He couldn't read her expression, but he had the uncomfortable sensation that she saw entirely too much when she looked at him.

As was often the case, Bobbie dominated the dinner conversation. Trevor loved his mother and knew she had a kind heart and a generous nature, but he wasn't blind to her bossiness or her penchant for being a little overbearing. While there were a few people who couldn't stand her, most folks overlooked her shortcomings in favor of her many good qualities. She'd been teaching in elementary school since before Trevor was born, and few questioned her competence—or her knack for running the most efficient and well-behaved classrooms in the school.

At the moment, she was on a diatribe about an incident that had happened to her through the locally owned bank where Emily had worked for several years, before quitting to be a full-time mother.

"All this new technology that's supposed to make things easier for the customers—it's just a lot of garbage," Bobbie said bluntly. "I called yesterday to see if a check had cleared, and I spent forty-five minutes on the telephone with some girl giving me directions on how to use the new automated teller service. I told her I don't want to talk to a recorded teller, and she said I had to learn how, because it would be much more 'convenient' for me in the long run. I want to know what's 'convenient' about having to punch in a half-dozen code numbers and then listen to a recording I can hardly understand, hmm? *She* could have given me the information I needed in less than five minutes. Laziness, that's what it is. No one wants to provide personal service anymore."

"The automated teller system really isn't that complicated once you learn it, Aunt Bobbie," Emily responded, but even she didn't look particularly convinced by her words.

"'Automated teller.'" The very term seemed to enrage Bobbie. "I'll tell you the same as I told that girl. If everything's going to be automated down there, why do they need a staff?"

"She's got a point there, Emily," Wade murmured, seeming to enjoy his wife's discomfort.

Having gotten her complaint out of her system, Bobbie abruptly changed the subject. "I talked to Arnette Lynch yesterday," she said, looking at Jamie as she mentioned the recently retired high-school drama teacher.

"How is her husband?" Jamie inquired politely.

"Still very weak from his chemotherapy treatments, I'm afraid, but Arnette said she thought he was feeling a bit better. She's confident she made the right decision in retiring."

"I'm sure she did."

"I'm so glad you were available to take her place. The students are thrilled to have a real theater veteran teaching them."

"I enjoy working with young actors," Jamie responded. "They're so eager and energetic. And some of them are quite talented."

"What does talent have to do with casting an Honoria High School production?" Emily asked dryly. "Mrs. Lynch always gave the lead roles to the students from the most prominent local families, regardless of whether they could act or sing."

Bobbie frowned. "That's not a very kind thing to say, Emily."

"But it's true, Aunt Bobbie. I saw the performance of *West Side Story* last fall, remember? Mayor Mc-Quade's strawberry-blond, freckled daughter Joannie played Maria. No way did she look Puerto Rican—and the poor girl couldn't act her way out of a paper bag."

"Couldn't sing worth a flip, either," Caleb muttered. "Sounded like a cat with its tail caught in a wringer. It was all I could do to sit through the whole show—and that was only because Bobbie had a death grip on my arm to keep me from leaving."

"Mrs. Lynch cast the popular, socially prominent kids back when *I* was in high school," Trevor agreed bluntly. "Everyone always knew who would have the best roles—and they were rarely the best qualified."

Jamie nodded somberly. "You never saw *me* hold the lead role at good ol' HHS, did you?"

Trevor thought he heard a touch of old resentment in her voice.

"I was always lucky to get a few lines," she continued, "even though Mrs. Lynch told me several times that she thought I had real talent."

Wade, who'd moved to Honoria only a couple of years earlier, looked startled. "If she thought you had talent, how did she justify not giving you better roles?"

Jamie shrugged, and Trevor suspected there was a world of emotion hidden behind her matter-of-fact tone. "She said she would face too much controversy if she tried to buck the established system. She was afraid it would cut into her contributions and jeopardize her ability to fund her productions. She knew my folks wouldn't put up a fuss if I was slighted—

unlike, say, the O'Briens or some of the other local society leaders."

Wade scowled. "Sounds like it was long past time for her to retire."

"She did the best she could," Bobbie said in defense of her colleague. "You know how difficult it can be to challenge the established order, Wade. You've had your share of criticism because you refuse to look the other way when some of the richer folks bend a few laws."

"The laws aren't any different for people with money than they are for people without," Wade said flatly.

Emily looked speculatively at Jamie. "I hear you're planning to do *Grease* in the spring. You know Joannie McQuade's going to demand the role of Sandy."

"None of my students will 'demand' a role—they'll audition," Jamie asserted. "If they're good, they'll get a part. If they show potential, I'll work with them until they're ready. If they show no glimmer of talent, I'll let them be extras, or assign them other responsibilities. There are a lot of interesting jobs in theater besides acting—lighting, set design and construction, sound, publicity, costumes, stage management."

"You'd make Joannie McQuade an extra?" Wide-eyed, Emily shook her head. "Her mother will be at the school to try to get you fired before you can say, 'Cut!'"

Trevor noted that Jamie didn't look notably intimidated. "I've spent seven years working in New York. I can handle Charlotte McQuade."

Emily made a balancing gesture with her hands.

"A city full of New Yorkers," she said, lowering one hand. "Charlotte McQuade," she continued, lowering the other. After considering it a moment, she shook her head wryly. "It's a close call, which is actually scarier."

"I'm sure Jamie can handle herself," Trevor commented.

The quick look she shot him expressed her appreciation—and perhaps a touch of surprise?

"I'm going to kindergarten," Sam announced to Jamie.

"In the fall, you mean?" she asked encouragingly.

He nodded.

"Are you excited?"

"I'm sort of scared," the boy admitted.

Trevor was a bit surprised. Sam didn't often share his feelings, especially with people he didn't know well. But he didn't usually take to new people as quickly as he had to Jamie, either.

"Don't be scared about school," Jamie encouraged. "For the most part, school is fun. Why else would I want to go back as a teacher?"

"Will you be *my* teacher?"

Jamie smiled and smoothed Sam's fair hair. "Not for a few years yet, Sammy. But whoever you get for a teacher, I'm sure you'll have a great year."

Trevor watched in resignation as his son fell a little deeper in love.

# 4

LATER THAT EVENING, the adults sat in the den, drinking coffee and talking while the children vied for attention. Sitting again on the couch beside Trevor, Jamie smiled at Abbie, then was surprised when the little girl reached out to her. Jamie obligingly took the toddler into her lap. Abbie immediately snatched for the heavy silver pendant Jamie wore.

"No, Abbie," Trevor said, reaching out to stop her. "You'll break it."

"She won't hurt it," Jamie assured him. "Trust me, it's not that fragile—or particularly valuable."

Trevor dropped his hand but she was aware that he kept a close eye on Abbie as she played with the pendant, babbling happily. Jamie really didn't mind the child playing with the necklace, but she prevented her several times from putting it in her mouth. She knew toddlers liked to taste things, but it just didn't seem like a particularly sanitary habit.

"Do you miss New York, Jamie?" Emily asked, distracting her for a moment.

"I miss the friends I made there, of course. I miss the theater—both as a performer and a patron. There was always something to do and someplace to go. Oh—and the food." She sighed nostalgically. "I'm not crazy about cooking for myself and I miss the convenience and variety of take-out food in New York. Honoria doesn't even have a decent Chinese delivery available, much less a really good deli."

"We've got pizza," Clay reminded her. "Sometimes Mom lets me order pizza for dinner. But not very often," he added wistfully.

"I like pizza, but I get tired of it if I have it too often," Jamie answered with a smile.

Clay looked disbelieving that anyone could ever grow tired of pizza.

"You'd never catch *me* living in a place like that," Bobbie said emphatically. "All that crime and rudeness and pollution—I simply can't see the appeal."

Jamie swallowed a chuckle at the stereotypes Bobbie so obviously believed. "It really isn't all that bad," she murmured. "By using simple common sense, I always felt quite safe."

Bobbie looked as skeptical as Clay had about the pizza.

Losing interest in the necklace, Abbie lurched forward to reach for one of Jamie's dangling silver earrings. Trevor and Jamie both made a grab for it and their hands collided, Trevor's covering Jamie's.

Jamie felt her stomach muscles contract. Trevor's skin felt unusually warm against hers. His fingers seemed to tighten almost reflexively around her hand.

Then they both suddenly snatched their hands away, giving Abbie an opportunity to take hold of the earring. Jamie winced when the baby gave an enthusiastic tug. "Better leave me some ear, Pumpkin," she said, disentangling Abbie's fingers. "I might need it sometime."

"Maybe I'd better take her," Trevor offered, starting to reach out.

Jamie shot him a frown. "Chill out, Trev. Abbie and I are getting along just fine, thank you."

Abbie laughed, as if she found Jamie's words hysterically funny. Trevor fell silent.

Sam tugged at Jamie's arm, looking jealous of the attention his sister was getting. "I got new shoes," he said, pointing to his sneakers. "I outgrewed my other ones."

"Did you?" Jamie tried to sound suitably impressed. "My goodness, you're growing fast."

"Daddy said he's going to put a brick on my head," the boy confided with a giggle. "I told him that was silly. I would still grow."

"Right. And you'd look rather silly walking around with a brick on your head all the time, wouldn't you?"

He laughed again and scooted an inch closer to her.

Having been asleep in a baby carrier on the floor at Wade's feet, little Claire began to squirm and fuss.

"We'd better be going," Emily said, rising. "As much as we've enjoyed the evening, it's time to get the kids bathed and in bed."

Clay didn't look overly enthused, Jamie noted in amusement, but he obediently gathered his electronic game and moved to stand with his family as the adults exchanged parting pleasantries. Still holding Abbie, Jamie remained seated for the moment, saying her goodbyes from the couch.

She agreed with Emily that they really should "do lunch" sometime—though she wondered if Emily was only making expected small talk, or the invitation was genuine. It wasn't as if they'd even known each other well when Jamie had lived here before. But then, Jamie hadn't known a lot of people. Her difficulties at home had kept her rather isolated from her peers.

The few close friends she'd had back then, like Susan, had implicitly understood that Jamie wouldn't be reciprocating their sleepover and birthday-party invitations, but she'd been aware that others had whispered among themselves about Jamie's alcoholic parents. Being a McBride, and the sister of a man wrongly suspected of murder, Emily surely knew the pain of being on the wrong side of the rumor mill. So maybe she and Jamie *could* be friends.

"As much fun as it is to hold this little cutie, I'd better be going, too," Jamie said only a few minutes after the Davenports had departed. She kissed Abbie's soft, chubby cheek, and then handed her to Trevor before rising and turning to Bobbie. "Thank you so much for having me to dinner, Mrs.—er, Bobbie," she said a bit self-consciously.

Bobbie stood and took her hand. "It was a pleasure to have you, dear. I know you want us to stop embarrassing you about it, but I need to thank you one last time for what you did at the swimming pool. None of us will ever forget it."

Aware that Trevor and Sam were standing behind her, Jamie murmured something appropriate and turned to Caleb.

"Good night, Jamie," he said, patting her arm in a fatherly manner. "You come back and see us sometime, you hear?"

"I would be delighted. Thank you."

"Trevor, walk Jamie to her car. I'll take Abbie." Bobbie reached for the child, assuming without waiting for confirmation that her instructions would be followed—as they usually were.

"I'll go, too," Sam said, starting forward.

His grandmother caught him by the shoulder. "No, sweetheart, you stay here with me and Grandpa. Say good-night to Ms. Flaherty now, and you'll see her again another time."

Pouting a little, Sam gazed up at Jamie. "Good night, Ms. Flaherty," he said, holding out his right hand as he'd seen the others do.

She shook his hand. "Good night, Sam. I'll see you around, okay?"

"I hope so," he answered wistfully.

Trevor motioned toward the doorway. "After you, Ms. Flaherty," he said with dry courtesy.

She gave him a cheeky grin. "Why, thank you, Mr. McBride. Good night again, everyone."

She happened to glance at Bobbie as she accompanied Trevor out of the room. The look on the older woman's face gave her pause for a moment. Just what *was* this, anyway? A gratitude dinner—or a fix-up?

Had Bobbie decided that Trevor had been in mourning long enough? And, if so, what on earth made Bobbie think *she* was a suitable match for a conservative lawyer with two small children?

"Mother's not particularly subtle," Trevor murmured as he and Jamie stepped into the still-warm evening air.

To avoid his eyes, she concentrated on admiring the stars spread so brightly above them, on the music of the night creatures singing in the woods surrounding the rural house, on the earth smells of early summer. As much as she'd enjoyed New York, she hadn't lost her appreciation for Georgia in June. "Your mother is very nice," she said, her tone deliberately absent.

"Yes, but she can be rather heavy-handed when she gets one of her nutty notions."

Deciding not to dance around the subject any longer, she turned to lean back against her car and study his face in the shadows. "And just what 'nutty notion' are you referring to, Trev?"

"My name," he reminded her, "is Trevor."

"Yes, I know. You were saying?"

"Surely you were aware that Mother's been nudging us toward each other all evening."

Jamie shrugged. "Since we were the only singles here this evening, it was only natural for her to encourage us to visit, I suppose."

"Maybe. But just in case she has something more in mind, I hope she doesn't cause you any embarrassment."

Chuckling, she ran a hand through her hair. "I don't embarrass easily."

"Why doesn't that surprise me?"

Sometimes Jamie just couldn't help herself. She reached out to stroke a fingertip along Trevor's firm, chiseled jaw. "How about you, Trev? Do you embarrass easily?"

She saw his eyes narrow in the yellow light coming from the overhead security pole. "Not usually," he drawled.

"Oh?" Still driven by her own personal imp, she walked her fingers up his chest until both her hands were resting on his shoulders. "Just what does it take to make you blush?"

He might have worn a very faint smile when he replied, "I haven't blushed since high school."

She fussed with his shirt collar, letting her fingers dip inside to lightly stroke his neck. "What was the cause then?"

"I believe it was a suggestion you made to me behind the gym."

She laughed at his dry tone. "And did you take me up on it?"

"No. I didn't have the nerve...then."

He was most definitely calling her bluff. Their mouths were only a couple of inches apart—and Jamie hoped her wry smile gave no clue to the way her heart was racing. "What about now?" she asked, the huskiness in her voice not entirely feigned.

"Now..." She felt his breath brush her lips, and her mouth tingled in anticipation. There was a momentary hesitation, and then Trevor drew back, slowly, breaking the contact between them. "I still don't have the nerve," he murmured.

She sighed in regret—and she was only partially teasing. "Pity."

He reached behind her to open the car door for her. "Drive carefully. And watch your speed."

"No problem," she quipped, pleased to note that her voice sounded steady—at least to her own ears. "I've tested my limits enough this evening, I think."

Trevor stepped back without answering. She slid into the car, started the engine and drove away. She glanced only once in the rearview mirror. Just long enough to see that Trevor was still standing there. Watching her.

HE COULD STILL FEEL her fingertips against his jaw. He could still feel the warmth of her lithe, vibrant body standing so close to his. He could still hear the echo of her husky laugh, like a brush of feathers against his nerve endings.

Trevor downed the single shot of bourbon he allowed himself each day and set the glass aside, his movements unhindered by the near-total darkness in the room. He was used to sitting in his living room alone in the dark, long after the children were in bed. Many nights he sat there resisting an urge to pour another drink—and brooding about Melanie. Remembering the satisfying, if somewhat unexciting, relationship he'd thought they had. Mourning the loss of the woman he had once loved and the illusions she had shattered. Facing a future that bore little resemblance to the one he'd envisioned when he had married her.

Tonight he found himself thinking of Jamie, instead.

It was still hard for him to believe how close he'd

come to acting like an awkward adolescent outside his parents' door earlier. He was a grown man, a widower, the father of two children, and still Jamie had brought him perilously near stammering incoherence—with only a brush of her fingers and that soft, sexy laugh. They seemed to have little more in common now than they'd had as teenagers—and yet he still found himself tempted to duck behind the high-school gym with her.

She had always had the strangest effect on him. He would have thought he'd outgrown it by now.

Apparently, he hadn't.

NEARLY EVERYONE in Honoria dined at Cora's Café, at least occasionally. One of the last establishments still thriving in the old section of downtown, it was within walking distance of city hall, the police station, the bank and a few small businesses, so the daily lunch trade was brisk.

Jamie was swept with nostalgia when she entered the café for lunch with her accountant on the Friday after her dinner with the McBrides. The place looked the same as it had fifteen years ago, she thought, looking around at the crowded tables with their red-and-white-checked coverings. The same cheap prints hung on the walls, though they were considerably more faded now, and the same old noisy cash register was still in use at the front checkout. No computerized register for this place—and they didn't take plastic.

Heavyset, frizzy-permed Mindy Hooper greeted Jamie at the door. Mindy had gone to work for Cora straight out of high school—almost ten years before Jamie's own graduation—and had been there ever since. She hadn't changed much during those years; now fast approaching forty, Mindy was slow-moving, broad-bottomed, plainspoken and apparently content with the sameness of her daily routine. "Hey, Jamie. I wondered when you were going to come see us again."

"It's good to be back, Mindy. Does Cora still make the best chocolate pie in the state?"

"Best chocolate pie in the world," Mindy replied, wryly patting her wide hip. "I'm waddling testimony to that."

Jamie laughed. "Is Clark Foster here yet? I'm meeting him for lunch."

"No, not yet. You go ahead and get a table and I'll send him your way when he comes in."

"Great. And when you get a minute, I'll have a glass of iced tea. It's already hot out."

"Just wait until summer really kicks in," Mindy predicted with cheery pessimism. "'Bout melted the dash in my car last August."

Since Georgians loved nothing more than complaining about the weather, Jamie murmured something sympathetic before heading for a nearby free table. She saw several people she knew, of course, and stopped on the way to exchange pleasantries. Cora's was almost as bad as the discount store when it came to being seen. Hardly a place for a discreetly anonymous tryst, she thought humorously as she took her seat. Not that there was anyone she was thinking of seeing on the sly at the moment, she added.

A balding, soft-middled businessman in his late thirties pulled out the chair across the table from her. "Sorry I'm late," he said. "Traffic was a bear."

She lifted an eyebrow. "Traffic? In Honoria?"

"Okay, it was old Mrs. Tucker," he admitted. "Driving five miles an hour right down the middle of Main Street."

She laughed. "Driving that big old car of hers? The one that looks as if it's driving itself because she's too short to be seen over the dashboard?"

"Yeah. She's had that car since before we were born, I think, and it might have all of twenty thousand miles on it by now."

"Most of them from driving down the middle of Main Street, right?"

"Exactly." He reached for one of the plastic-coated menus stuck between the paper-napkin dispenser and a wooden box holding salt, pepper, ketchup and pepper sauce. "You haven't ordered yet, have you?"

"No, I just got here. I did ask for iced tea...oh, here it is." She smiled up at Mindy, who unceremoniously plunked two mason jars full of iced tea in front of them.

"What'll y'all have?" Mindy asked without bothering with an order pad.

Clark glanced up from the menu. "What's today's special?"

"Same as it is every Friday. Chicken-fried steak with mashed potatoes, cream gravy, white beans and turnip greens, or fried catfish with coleslaw, hush puppies and green tomato relish."

Clark replaced the menu. "I'll have the chicken-fried steak."

"Very healthy choice, Clark," Jamie teased, having heard him complain more than once about his difficulty losing weight.

He sighed. "You're right. Add a green salad to that, will you, Mindy? With Thousand Island dressing."

Jamie chuckled and shook her head. "I don't suppose you have anything broiled or grilled, Mindy?"

"Got the diet plate. A fried hamburger patty, cottage cheese and canned peaches."

Cora's Café had been serving the same "diet plate" since the 1950s, despite changes in diet philosophies. Jamie conceded defeat and ordered the catfish.

When they were alone again, Clark laced his fingers together, rested his hands on the table and tried to look professional...which wasn't an easy task, considering his resemblance to the Pillsbury doughboy, Jamie thought with secret amusement. "I've gone over all your records and everything seems to be in order," he told her. "I've worked up figures for your estimated quarterly tax payments—the first one's due next week, by the way. I have your paperwork in my briefcase here at my feet. I'll give it to you after we've had our lunch."

She nodded. "I appreciate it, Clark. I was pretty sure everything was in order, but it's nice to have a professional opinion. It's too inconvenient for me to have an accountant in New York while I'm living in Honoria."

He looked a bit smug. "Your accounts are relatively easy to manage, but I agree that you need a professional to keep an eye on them. You invested wisely while you were in New York. You shouldn't have to worry about retirement."

She felt a surge of satisfaction at his words. He could have no idea, of course, how important it was for her to have a sense of security about money. She hadn't chosen a safe, predictable career path—acting was hardly a profession known for job security—but she had lived frugally and worked steadily as a substitute teacher between acting jobs. As impractical as she was in some ways, Jamie never fooled around when it came to money. She had no intention of ending up like her parents, a couple of aging alcoholics living hand-to-mouth on government checks.

It had been Clark who had suggested they have this meeting over lunch, telling her it was a nice, casual way to start off their business relationship. Jamie hadn't hesitated to accept, since she had few plans now that she was on summer break. Because she knew he was in the middle of a divorce, she didn't ask about his wife, but it wasn't difficult to get him talking about his two sons. She concentrated on her somewhat guilty enjoyment of the fried catfish while Clark liberally sprinkled pepper sauce on his greens and bragged about his boys.

They were almost finished with their meal when Trevor entered the café with his father. They paused at the table, Caleb speaking first. "Well, hello, Jamie. Clark, how's it going?"

"Pretty good, Caleb. How about you?"

"Oh, getting along."

Jamie glanced at Trevor and found him looking at

her with a frown. He quickly smoothed the expression, but she wondered why he'd looked so disapproving. She couldn't imagine what she'd done to annoy him. She'd thought they'd parted on good terms.

"Hello, Jamie," he said with a formal nod of greeting. His tone was noticeably cooler when he added, "Clark."

Clark's response could only be described as frigid. "Trevor."

Surprised by the obvious antagonism between the two men, Jamie speculated on what might have caused it. The McBrides were notorious for their local feuds, but, as far as she knew, there'd never been a problem between the McBrides and Clark's family. This must be something personal.

"How are the children, Trevor?" she asked in an effort to ease the tension a bit.

"They're fine, thank you."

"Have you found a new nanny yet?"

"Yes. I have one on a trial basis now."

"I hope she works out for you."

"Thanks. Dad, we'd better grab a table while there's one available. Mindy's been giving us the look."

"The one that says 'Sit your butts down so I can do my job'?" Caleb spoke from longtime experience with the no-nonsense waitress. "Guess we'd better cooperate. Good to see you, Jamie. And you, too, Clark."

"Enjoy your lunch," Clark replied politely, his smile forced.

Trevor left with only a vague nod toward Jamie.

She feigned a shiver. "Did it suddenly get cold in here?"

Clark had returned his attention to his plate, his appetite obviously little affected by the interruption. "Trevor and I have had a few disagreements lately."

"Gee, I never would have guessed."

"He's representing my wife in the divorce," Clark admitted. "I think he's doing so a bit more fiercely than necessary. I've accused him of trying to bankrupt me. He gives me a slick line about how he's just doing what she's hired him to do."

Jamie grimaced. "Sorry. I didn't know."

"I always liked Trevor, though I didn't know him very well. But that was before I saw him in cutthroat-lawyer mode."

"Trevor's always been an overachiever. I'm sure he just figures he's giving his client her money's worth."

"Yeah, well, I'm starting to take it personally. Valerie and I were handling things fairly civilly until the lawyers got involved—especially Trevor."

"It's always sad when a marriage breaks up."

He sighed and Jamie saw a flash of what might have been guilt cross his face before he muttered, "Especially when there are kids involved. I really hate this for my boys."

Without knowing—or even wanting to know—the details of the breakup, Jamie offered a simple, "I'm sorry, Clark." She knew from personal observation how ugly divorces could become, and how easily innocent bystanders could be caught in the middle. She intended to be very careful not to become involved in this one, in any way. Not even by asking questions.

He nodded his gratitude, then changed the subject. "Want any dessert? Cora still makes those great pies with the mile-high meringue."

"As much as I love her pies, I'm afraid I'll have to pass. I'm too full. But feel free to have some yourself."

Reluctantly, Clark looked at his own thoroughly cleaned plate. "I guess I'd better pass, too. I've already gone way over my limit for today."

Ten minutes later, Jamie made her way out of the bustling diner, the paperwork tucked beneath her arm. She didn't look back at Trevor's table, but she had the oddest sensation that she was being watched as she and Clark left the restaurant.

# 5

JAMIE WAS PAINTING when her telephone rang that evening. Still holding her brush in one hand, her eyes focused assessingly on the lake-and-forest scene taking shape in front of her, she reached with her left hand for the cordless phone she'd placed nearby. "Hello?"

"It's Trevor."

That took her attention away from the canvas. "Well, hey, Trev," she drawled, masking her surprise. "What's up?"

"I, er, just thought I'd call and say hi. I suppose you thought I was rather short at the diner earlier."

She leaned back on her stool. "You do take your job seriously, don't you, Counselor? One might have thought you were facing poor Clark from the opposite side of a courtroom, rather than in Cora's Café."

"Poor Clark?" He obviously didn't care for the term. "I hardly think that description fits."

"I really don't know the particulars of his divorce, and I'd just as soon not hear them. Clark's my accountant, and the details of his personal life don't concern me." Once again, she remembered what a mess she'd found herself in the last time she'd offered comfort and friendship to a man in the middle of a divorce.

"Just watch yourself around him, okay? That squeaky-clean choirboy image he puts on doesn't quite give the full picture."

"Are you telling me I shouldn't trust him as my accountant?" she asked bluntly.

After only a momentary hesitation, Trevor conceded, "No. I have no reason to believe there's anything questionable about his work."

"Then that's all that matters, isn't it? Nothing else is really relevant to me."

"So your lunch with him was strictly business?"

"You could say that," she agreed coolly. "*My* business."

She could almost hear him wince. "Look, Jamie, I didn't mean to sound intrusive," he said awkwardly. "It's just—well, you haven't been back in town very long and you probably aren't aware of some of the things that go on around here."

"Honoria hasn't changed that much while I was away. And I know how to plug in to the gossip lines—if I had any interest in doing so."

"I didn't call to gossip." He sounded annoyed by the implication.

"Then why *did* you call?" she challenged him.

"I want you to have dinner with me tomorrow night."

Jamie nearly dropped her paintbrush. She had to call on her acting skills to respond with cool amusement to his tactless invitation. "Was that a request—or an order?"

"A request," he replied, his tone a bit rueful. "I'm sorry if I sounded abrupt. I'm afraid I'm out of practice when it comes to this sort of thing. It's been a few years since I asked a woman to dinner."

A few *years*? Had he really not been on a date since his wife died? Not quite sure how she felt about that, Jamie considered the invitation.

Whatever his reason for asking, it was only dinner, she reminded herself. Her longtime fascination with Trevor made her want to accept—but also made her wary of doing so. She was just starting to feel comfortable in town again. She was hesitant to risk firing up the gossips with an experiment that would probably end up going nowhere.

She had told herself repeatedly that she'd come back to rest, to teach, to put painful old memories to rest, and to decide what to do with the rest of her life now that she had accepted that her acting career had gone about as far as she was willing to take it. She had tried to convince herself that it was only coincidence that she'd decided to take the teaching job only after hearing that Trevor McBride had moved back to Honoria. But she'd always been aware of a nagging urge to see him again, this man who'd haunted her dreams and her memories for so long. The man to whom other men had never quite measured up, no matter how hard she had tried not to compare them to him.

"We could drive into Atlanta for dinner," Trevor said, correctly guessing a small part of the reason for her hesitation. "That way we wouldn't have to worry about whatever Martha Godwin or any of the other local jaw-flappers around here might say about seeing us together."

She was relieved by his suggestion. "That sounds nice," she said.

There never had been any question, really, that she would turn him down. She had waited too long for this.

"Shall I pick you up at seven?"

"Pick me up?" She slid comfortably back into teasing, using it, as always, as a way to hide her real emotions. "Shouldn't we meet in a dark alley somewhere?"

"No. But I'll wear a disguise, if you like."

His dry rejoinder pleased her. "How will I recognize you?"

"I'll wear a pink rose on my lapel."

"A pink rose?" She laughed. "That should serve as an effective disguise in itself, given your ultra-conservative-attorney image."

"Then it will serve its purpose, won't it? If anyone sees it, they'll assume I'm one of your eccentric theater friends."

"What makes you think my theater friends are eccentric?"

"Call it a wild guess. I'll see you tomorrow evening."

"I'll be working on my own disguise," she promised.

"I shudder to think what that might be." But she thought she heard a smile in his voice. "Good night, Jamie."

She hung up the phone and looked back at the painting. Might as well clean her brushes, she thought. She doubted that she would be able to concentrate any more tonight.

TREVOR WAS COMBATTING guilt when he turned into Jamie's driveway Saturday evening. As much as the kids enjoyed staying with their grandparents, he still felt badly about leaving them on a weekend after spending so many hours away from them while he worked during the week. It hadn't been easy for him to ask his mother to baby-sit, especially since he'd had to explain his reason for needing her. To her credit, Bobbie's only reaction when he'd told her he was taking Jamie to dinner was to tell him to have a good time.

Whether she had said so or not, he knew his mother was pleased. She'd been urging him to get out more for the past five or six months. She'd said it "wasn't natural" for a young man like him to spend so much time alone. When he'd reminded her that he had two young children to raise, she had replied that she thought he was a very good father, but he still needed a life of his own. Melanie, she had added as gently as possible for her, would not have wanted him to spend the rest of his life in mourning.

He wondered what she would have said if he'd told her he suspected Melanie might have taken great satisfaction from having him do exactly that. Trevor still hadn't told anyone, including his parents, the full story surrounding his wife's death. Bobbie couldn't know that he had been dealing with a great deal more than grief during the eleven months that had passed since the accident.

He had quickly realized that Washington, D.C., was no place for him to come to grips with what had happened—or for him to raise his children alone. He hadn't wanted his kids to hear the gossip about Melanie, or to be told just what their mother had been doing when she'd supposedly been involved in all her charitable activities. He had needed his family, a change of scenery and the company of people who had barely known Melanie and hadn't heard the rumors that had sped like wildfire through the ranks of his D.C. colleagues. He had found all of that here.

But he hadn't expected to find Jamie Flaherty, or to be drawn to her as strongly as he had been in the past. This time, he'd decided, there weren't as many reasons for him to try to resist her. As long as he was careful not to let himself get too deeply involved—as long as he made sure his children weren't affected by his actions—there was no reason he couldn't take Jamie up on some of the things she seemed to be offering. Things he had decided he wanted very badly.

They were both young, single, and had only recently moved back to town. He doubted that footloose Jamie was interested in a long-term commitment to a single father, which didn't particularly disturb him since he wasn't looking for that, either. At this point, he had no plans to marry again—to ever trust another woman with his heart and, most importantly, with his children. As for Jamie, he would actually be surprised if she stayed for the entire school year. As flighty as she seemed to be, she'd probably take off as soon as she had an acting offer. Either that, or she'd get bored again with small-town life and head back for the excitement of the Big Apple.

But in the meantime...

He parked his car and reached for the gift he had brought her on impulse.

Trevor had considered himself quite accomplished in the Washington social scene. He'd mingled with politicians, celebrities, business moguls, heads of state. He'd spent almost as much time in tuxedos as he had in casual wear and there had rarely been a time when he'd felt awkward or tongue-tied. But when Jamie Flaherty opened her door wearing a slim-fitting, shoulder-baring, leg-revealing, yellow sundress, he almost forgot his own name.

If she noticed his poleaxed expression, she gave no sign of it. "Hey, Trev. Nice tie."

Since he had no idea whether she was serious or mocking his conservative tastes, he settled for a simple, "Thanks. You look...nice."

"Why, thank you." She slanted a look up at him that left little doubt that she was laughing at him.

Resigning himself to an evening of Jamie's style of teasing, he held out the single pink rose he'd brought her. "I was going to wear this, but it clashed with my shirt."

She accepted the perfect bloom with a smile. "Thank you again. It's lovely. I'll put it in a vase to keep it fresh. I would wear it, but it clashes with my hair."

He glanced at her short, saucy cut. "When did you go red?"

"Last year—after my brunette stage, which came after my blond phase. I get bored easily."

Which pretty much confirmed what he'd been thinking. "Red must be a popular color these days. My sister keeps her hair that color now, too—though it's more of a strawberry blond than yours. It took me a while to get used to it, but I like it now."

"Tara dyed her hair?" Jamie seemed surprised. "I can't picture her as anything but blond."

"She looks good either way."

"I'm sure she does. Tara's always been beautiful. Would you like a drink or something before we go?" she asked after placing the rose in a crystal bud vase.

Having a drink meant spending more time here with Jamie. In her house. Alone. With her in that body-skimming, flirty little dress. He didn't think he could take that, yet. "No. If you're ready, we'll go."

She reached for her purse. "Then I suppose I'm ready."

At least it appeared he would keep her amused this evening. He supposed that was something.

TREVOR DIDN'T have to worry about making conversation during the hour-long drive to the restaurant he'd selected in Atlanta. Jamie talked the entire way, telling him about the acting roles she'd had in New York, and sharing stories about some of the celebrities she'd met. It was almost as if she was trying to fill the awkward silences between them.

He didn't mind her chattering. Trying to keep up with her conversational gymnastics kept him from dwelling on the way her skirt had ridden up on her thighs. The way her seat belt pulled the top of her dress so tightly against her breasts. Her faint, intriguingly citrusy scent.

He shifted in his seat, annoyed with himself for letting his hormones run away with him. Just because he hadn't been to bed with a woman during the past year didn't mean he couldn't control himself for an evening.

The rather one-sided conversation continued during the excellent dinner they were served at a cozily secluded table in a quiet corner of the elegant restaurant. Jamie seemed as comfortable in their posh surroundings as she did curled on the sofa at her house, making him wonder if she *ever* felt awkward. If she did, he certainly couldn't tell.

"I've done enough gabbing," she said when they had almost finished their meal. "Why don't you tell me about your adventures in Washington? I bet you've met some very interesting people."

"A few."

"Tell me about some of the things you've seen," she said, studying him across the tiny table. "Entertain me while I savor my dessert."

Though he wasn't sure exactly what it would take to entertain her, he managed to come up with a few anecdotes. Jamie seemed to find them amusing, though he was aware he could not quite match her flair for storytelling.

"Now tell me the latest cute things your kids have done," she demanded when he'd run out of innocuous Washington stories. "You've hardly mentioned them this evening."

He smiled wryly. "I didn't think talking about one's kids was proper date etiquette. I could be wrong. Last time I was out on a date, I didn't even *have* kids."

"Didn't you and your wife go out on dates?"

He felt a muscle tense in the back of his neck. "Yes, of course we went out. I was referring to dates in the traditional sense."

Her eyes searched his face, making him wonder what she saw there. "Did your wife like the D.C. social scene?"

More than he had ever realized, Trevor could have answered. As far as he had known, she'd been content to stay at home in the evenings with him and the children, which was what he had generally preferred when they had no pressing engagements. He hadn't known, of course, that she'd found her own entertainment during the hours he had spent at the office. He merely nodded in response to Jamie's question.

"And did you?" she asked.

"It got old fast." Though his appetite was gone, he took another bite of his cheesecake, just to give him something to do for a moment.

Her curiosity had not yet been satisfied. "Have you decided to stay in Honoria permanently now, or will you go back to Washington eventually?"

"I have no plans to go back. My father's been working twelve-hour days long enough. He's needed a partner for several years. When he's ready to retire, I'll take over the practice."

"Handling divorces and bankruptcies in Honoria is a lot different from dealing with affairs of state in the nation's capital. Are you sure it's enough for you?"

"I'm confident it will be, especially combined with the responsibility of raising my kids."

"Tell me about the new nanny. Do the children like her?"

"Her name is Sarah Brown. She moved to town last year with her husband, who works at O'Brien's Lumberyard. Their only son is in college now, but Sarah likes kids and enjoys taking care of them. I wanted someone more mature this time, and she came highly recommended. Abbie's taken to her easily enough—but then, Abbie likes everybody."

"She's such a sweetheart. What about Sam? Has he taken to Sarah, too?"

Trevor had to make an effort not to sigh. "Sam doesn't accept newcomers into his life easily. It seems that his shyness grows worse with time rather than better."

"I haven't noticed him being overly shy."

"That's because he isn't with you. He took to you right away." And Trevor still couldn't quite explain it—except to decide that whatever magic Jamie worked on him was equally potent to his son.

"He's an adorable little boy, Trev. So bright and observant. And Abbie's an angel. You're doing a wonderful job with them."

Trevor was surprised by how much her words touched him. "Thanks," he said, his tone gruffer than he'd intended. "I'm doing my best. And I have a lot of help from my parents. Mother can be a handful at times, but she's been an enormous help to me with the kids."

"I'm sure she has. Bobbie is one of the most efficient and competent people I've ever met."

"Not to mention the bossiest," Trevor added with affectionate irony.

Jamie laughed softly. "That, too. What about the children's other grandparents? Do they get to see them often?"

Trevor's smile faded. "My wife's mother passed away several years ago. Her father is still living, but in poor health. We see him very rarely."

The young man who'd served them all evening appeared at the table with a carafe in his hand. "More coffee, folks?"

Trevor and Jamie both accepted the offer. Trevor, for one, was in no hurry to leave. However, he had not planned to spend so much time talking about his children. And certainly not about Melanie, or her family. He'd intended to keep this evening strictly between himself and Jamie.

"What about you?" he asked, watching her sip her coffee. "Has talking about New York this evening given you a yen to go back?"

"I'll go back to New York—if for nothing more than holiday visits. But for now, I'm content where I am. I'm spending the summer resting, painting, catching up on my reading, making new friends in town. And I'm really looking forward to starting the new school year, and putting together my own productions from scratch."

"Painting?" he asked, zeroing in on that one word.

"Yes. I've always enjoyed working with oils on canvas, but I haven't had much time for it during the past few years. I'm certainly no great artist, but it's a pleasant hobby."

"I'd like to see your work."

"Why, certainly. I would love to show you my work," she almost purred, giving him a heavy-lidded look over her coffee cup. "And maybe I'll show you my paintings sometime, too."

Damn it, she'd done it again. Caught him off guard with a sexy laugh, a sizzling look and a blatant innuendo. Someday soon he just might surprise her and call her bluff when she got in one of these teasing moods. He wondered if she would still laugh at him then.

The niggling thought that she just might made him scowl.

Her laughter rippled through him again. "Poor Trevvie. Have I embarrassed you again?"

He leveled a look at her across the table. "You may call me Trevor, or Trev, if you insist. But I'll be damned if I answer to 'Trevvie.'"

"I'll try not to forget that," she promised, her eyes dancing.

"See that you don't."

To his relief, she dropped the flirting and started talking about a controversial new ordinance the Honoria city council was considering. It didn't particularly surprise him that she could switch that quickly from foolishness to small-town politics. Trevor had never questioned Jamie's intelligence. And if there was one thing he had learned to expect from her, it was the unexpected.

TREVOR DEBATED with himself for less than a minute when Jamie invited him in at her door. His mother was keeping the kids overnight—"just so you won't have to disturb them if you come in late," she had assured him—so there wasn't any need for him to rush home. It couldn't hurt to have just one last cup of coffee, he thought.

"Make yourself comfortable," Jamie said, waving a hand toward the couch as she headed for the kitchen. "I'll be back in a few minutes."

She glanced over her shoulder, a by-now-familiar gleam in her eyes. "Feel free to loosen your tie, if you like."

He should probably be pleased that he kept her amused, he thought in resignation, taking off his jacket and tossing it over the back of a chair. He supposed that was better than boring her.

Jamie noticed his missing jacket and loosened tie as she carried the two steaming mugs of coffee into the room. She nodded approval.

"Better?" he asked wryly.

Setting the mugs on the coffee table, she straightened and eyed him consideringly. "There's just one more thing," she murmured, taking a step toward the end of the couch where he sat.

He watched her warily. "And that is...?"

"This." Before he'd guessed her intentions, she pounced on him, rumpling his formerly tidy dark blond hair with both hands. He could feel it tousled on his forehead when she had finished. "There," she said in satisfaction. "I've been wanting to do that for ages."

She started to back away, but Trevor caught her wrist and gave a sharp tug, tumbling her onto his lap. "I've been wanting to do *this* for ages," he muttered, then covered her mouth with his.

The last time he had kissed Jamie Flaherty, she had been a high-spirited, fifteen-year-old girl just discovering her feminine attributes. He'd been a serious, studious eighteen-year-old with little experience at that sort of thing. Kissing her then had sent his raging hormones skyrocketing, had made his heart slam against his chest and his pulse roar in his ears.

Almost fifteen years later, she still had the same effect on him.

Her lips were full. Soft. Warm. Eager. Her slender body fit into his arms as easily as if she'd been custom-designed to his specifications. There was no hesitation when she returned the kiss, no coy holding back. No sign of surprise at his actions.

Perhaps he'd meant to shake her composure, the way she'd been unnerving him all evening. But once again, he was the one caught off guard, thoroughly bemused and mesmerized by her.

Fifteen *decades* of experience could not have prepared him for Jamie Flaherty.

When the long kiss ended, she had one hand resting on his cheek, the other arm around his neck. Her smile looked a bit smug, but he had the satisfaction of seeing a glazed expression in her eyes—at least until she lowered her lids and hid her reaction from him.

It was nice to think that maybe, just once, he had managed to rattle her a little.

"Why, Trev," she said, her voice a shade huskier than usual. "Was that an impulsive action?"

"I've been known to indulge in them occasionally."

She slid her fingertips across his mouth. "You should do so more often."

"Maybe you're right." He pulled her toward him again.

The second kiss was no less spectacular than the first. Trevor was startled again by his own reactions to it—the rush of heat, the surge of hunger, the ache of need. Maybe he'd managed to be satisfied with a few stolen kisses in the past, but he knew it would never be enough now. Not if he stayed here much longer with Jamie curled in his lap, her arms around him, her mouth moving so willingly beneath his.

Because he allowed his impulses to lead him only so far, he brought the kiss to an end.

Jamie studied his face for a moment, then slid off his lap to sit beside him on the couch. "The coffee's getting cold," she said, her voice as matter-of-fact as if nothing had just occurred between them.

Trevor dragged his gaze from her moist, kiss-darkened lips. "I think I'll skip the coffee, if you don't mind," he said, trying to imitate her casual attitude. "It's getting late."

"All right. Thanks for dinner."

He couldn't tell if she was at all disappointed that he was leaving. Resigned to never knowing exactly what she was thinking, he stood and took a step backward—out of the reach of temptation. "Good night."

.She rose gracefully. "Say hi to the kids for me."

He nodded, though he didn't plan to say much to his children—especially Sam—about Jamie. He still didn't really expect this thing between them to go anywhere, and he didn't want the children's lives to be disrupted again when it ended.

She walked him to the door and opened it for him. "Good night, Trev."

Before he could respond, he found himself on the other side of the closed door. Even as he drove away, he knew he would be spending part of the night sitting in his darkened living room, thinking about Jamie.

It bothered him that he didn't know whether he would even cross her mind now that he was out of her sight.

ALMOST AS IF there was a chance he could see though her door, Jamie waited until the sound of Trevor's car engine had faded completely before she dropped limply onto the couch and pressed a hand over her heart. It was still racing—a fact she had made a massive effort to disguise from Trevor.

That buttoned-down, clean-cut, quiet-spoken lawyer certainly could kiss—even better than he had when they were teenagers.

He hadn't said anything about seeing her again. She understood it must be difficult for him to spend time away from the children—something she'd never had to deal with before, since she'd never dated a single father. As a matter of fact, she'd always made it a rule not to get involved with men who had children.

She'd never wanted that extra complication in her previous relationships. Her few romances had been complicated enough without having to worry about the tender sensibilities of innocent children.

For Trevor, though, she was inclined to bend her rules.

Besides, she liked Trevor's kids. Abbie was adorable and Sam—well, she had a serious soft spot for little Sam.

Maybe dating a guy with kids wouldn't be so bad, after all. Especially when that guy was Trevor McBride—a man she had been fantasizing about for almost as long as she could remember.

# 6

JAMIE WAS SITTING by the pool again on Tuesday afternoon, feigning interest in a paperback and trying to look as if she was enjoying herself. Okay, she thought, so maybe summer vacation wasn't so great. So maybe she was bored out of her mind.

The problem was that she simply wasn't accustomed to having time to herself. She'd worked steadily in New York—in one job or another. Even in high school, she had worked every summer, both for the money and to avoid spending time at home. Now that she had several weeks ahead of her with nothing in particular to do—well, she didn't know how to entertain herself.

Maybe she should take a vacation or something. It would certainly beat sitting at home waiting for the phone to ring—something else she wasn't used to doing. She started when someone suddenly laid a hand on her arm. Looking quickly around, she relaxed with a smile. "Why, hello, Sam."

He gave her a shy smile from beneath his fringe of blond bangs. "Hi, Jamie."

"How have you been?"

"Okay. What are you reading?"

She glanced at the paperback. "It's a mystery story."

"Is it good?"

"I've read better."

"You can read my Berenstein Bears books. They're all good."

"Thank you, Sam. I'm sure I'd like that much better."

"They're at my house. You'd have to come there to borrow them."

It was the second time he had invited her to his house. She wondered again how Trevor would react if he knew. She looked around, seeing no one who seemed particularly interested in Sam's whereabouts. "Are you here with your nanny?"

Looking suddenly guilty, Sam shook his head. "No. Mrs. Brown's home with Abbie. Abbie's taking a nap."

"Then who brought you to the pool?"

"I did," he answered simply.

Jamie swung her legs to the side of the lounge chair and pushed herself upright. "You mean you came here *alone*? Surely you didn't have permission for that."

The boy looked down at his sneakers. "I'm s'posed to be taking a nap, too. But I didn't *want* to take a nap. I wanted to come see you."

"How did you know I would be here?"

"I hoped you would."

"Sam, I have to take you home," Jamie said, standing and reaching for the black mesh cover-up that matched her black bikini. "Your nanny is probably frantic by now."

Just the thought of little Sam walking the five

blocks or so from his house alone, crossing streets and risking getting hit by a car, or lost, or who-knew-what, made Jamie's blood run cold.

"I don't want to go home. Can't I stay here with you? I'll be good."

It wasn't easy to resist his damp eyes and quivering lip, but Jamie held firm. "I have to take you home, Sam. Maybe we can get there before Mrs. Brown realizes you're gone."

"I don't like her. She talks to me like I'm a little kid."

Jamie knew better than to remind him that he was, in fact, a little kid. His hand seemed so tiny when he slipped it into hers. "I'm sure she means well, Sammy. Maybe she just hasn't spent much time lately with big five-year-old boys like you."

"Have you spent time with boys like me?"

"Well...no," she admitted. "Not much."

"I like it when *you* talk to me."

"Thank you. We'll have a nice long talk soon, okay? But first let's get you home so Mrs. Brown won't be worried about you."

He sighed heavily. "Okay."

Sliding her feet into black, cork-soled flip-flops, she led him toward the pool exit.

"Don't forget your book," he reminded her, looking back over his shoulder.

"I'll leave it for someone who might like it better than I did."

She knew where Trevor lived, of course, though she hadn't actually been there. As small as Honoria was, it hadn't been hard to discreetly find out which house he'd moved into. Sam said very little during the walk home, but he didn't try to resist again. He and Jamie spotted Trevor's car in the driveway at the same time.

"Uh-oh. Daddy's home."

Jamie tightened her hand reassuringly around the child's suddenly cold fingers. "Mrs. Brown probably called him. We'd better let him know you're all right, okay?"

"He's gonna be mad," Sam predicted glumly.

"Yes. He probably will be. But he'll get over it...if you promise never to do anything like this again."

The front door opened before Sam could answer. Wearing a grim expression and carrying his daughter on his hip, Trevor came out of the house, followed by a distraught-looking middle-aged woman. Jamie could almost feel the panic emanating from them. "Trevor."

He turned, spotted her, then dropped his gaze to Sam. The expression that crossed his face brought a lump to Jamie's throat. He recovered quickly, but not before she saw the full, weak-kneed extent of his relief at seeing his son safe.

"Sam." He stepped swiftly toward them. "Where have you been?"

"I went to the pool to see Jamie," the boy muttered.

"Without asking anyone? Without telling anyone you were leaving?"

Sam hung his head even lower.

"Sam!" Abbie squealed, waving a chubby hand at her brother.

"How did he know you were at the pool?" Trevor asked, turning to Jamie. "Have you two talked?"

Something in his voice made her frown. "No, of course not. He just took a chance at finding me there—and, fortunately, I was."

"Go up to your room, Sam. I'll be in to talk to you soon."

Sam looked up at his father in protest, his hand tightening around Jamie's. "But I want to show Jamie my—"

"You'd better mind your dad, Sammy," she murmured quickly. "I don't think he's in a mood to argue with you."

"Definitely not." Trevor jerked his chin toward the house. "Your room, Sam."

Jamie had to bite her lip to keep from suggesting to Trevor that he might go a little easier on the boy. Sam looked so small and sad as he trudged into the house. But it was none of her business, she reminded herself. What Sam had done was *very* wrong, and it was important that he learn never to do anything like that again. And, besides, she knew very well that what Trevor really wanted to do was snatch the boy into his arms and hold on to him.

"I'll take Abbie in, if you like, Mr. McBride," the nanny offered, looking nervously at her stern employer.

Trevor nodded and handed over the always-cheerful tot. "I'll be in shortly, Mrs. Brown. I'd like to talk to you."

Jamie watched her swallow. "Yes, sir."

Waiting only until the nanny had followed Sam

into the house, Jamie pointed a finger at Trevor. "*Don't* fire her."

"She's already fired," Trevor answered flatly. "I just haven't had a chance to tell her yet."

Jamie felt like throwing up her hands in exasperation. "Honestly, Trev, if you insist on perfection in a nanny, you'll never keep one more than a couple of weeks. *Everyone* makes mistakes."

"She never even heard him leave the house."

"I'm sure she was busy. Maybe Abbie woke up, or something. And you're underestimating your son. Sam is a very smart little boy. All you need to do is warn Mrs. Brown to keep that in mind from now on. I'm sure she'll be extra-vigilant with him in the future."

"How can you be sure?" he challenged. "You don't even know her."

"She looked nice."

"Oh, well, *that* changes everything."

"I know you were worried, but there's no need for sarcasm."

"Worried?" His rigid shoulders suddenly sagged. "Damn it, Jamie, I was petrified."

Softening, she took a step toward him and laid a hand on his arm. "I know you were. I saw it in your eyes."

"Sarah was almost hysterical when she called me. I must have flown here—I hardly remember the drive. A dozen possibilities were running through my head—and none of them were good."

"Trevor, I know. But Sam's fine."

"If you hadn't been at the pool..."

"But I was, thank goodness. And I made him promise never to do anything like that again."

"I'll make sure he doesn't."

"Yes. But—"

He studied her face from beneath half-lowered lashes. "But what?"

"Just remember he's only five," she couldn't resist saying.

"I know how to raise my son."

His tone was cool. Distant. It was hard to believe this was the same man who had kissed her senseless on her couch. "I'm sure you do. I'm just very fond of Sam."

Her hand was still resting on his arm. Though he'd shown no sign of noticing it, he stepped away, breaking the contact between them. "Thank you for rescuing my son for a second time, Jamie. It seems my family is in your debt once again."

For some reason, he sounded more annoyed than grateful. "Don't be ridiculous. All I did was walk him home."

"And I appreciate it. Would you like me to give you a lift? You can't be comfortable walking around dressed like that."

Her cover-up was almost as concealing as the short T-shirt dresses she often wore in the summer. Only a hint of her bikini was visible through the fine black mesh. She was perfectly comfortable walking around this way. "You have things to take care of here. I'll be fine."

"You're sure?"

"I'm sure." She was beginning to get irritated, herself. She knew Trevor had been through a stressful ordeal, but she saw no reason for him to suddenly treat her like a passing acquaintance. It wasn't as if she'd done anything to cause his problem with his son—even if Sam had used her for an excuse for going AWOL.

"I'll call you," Trevor said as she started away.

She wasn't appeased. "For another thank-you dinner? Don't bother."

"Jamie..."

"Goodbye, Trevor."

He didn't try to detain her when she turned and walked briskly away. He hadn't just annoyed her, she realized as she walked through her front door some fifteen minutes later. He had actually hurt her feelings. She hadn't fully realized until now that he still had the power to do that to her. And she didn't like it at all.

IT WAS A LONG EVENING in Trevor's household, but the children were finally in bed, and Trevor had time alone to reflect on the afternoon's events. Standing at the window of his darkened living room, a drink in his hand, he looked out at the quiet neighborhood in which he had chosen to settle his family. It was 10:00 p.m., and many of the other houses were already dark. His hardworking neighbors tended to be the early-to-bed, early-to-rise types.

He would bet that Jamie, like him, was still awake.

Jamie. He had only to close his eyes to picture her clearly, standing outside his house the way she had earlier. Her dark red hair had gleamed like polished copper in the afternoon sun. Her gold-flecked green eyes had glittered with rapidly changing emotions. Her long, slender legs had stretched endlessly beneath the hem of her short cover-up, and the tantalizing glimpses of bikini through the mesh had almost cleared his mind of coherent thought a time or two.

He'd had to make an enormous effort to keep his reactions to her hidden. Maybe he'd done so a bit too effectively. He'd had the distinct impression that she had been miffed with him when she'd stalked away.

Truth was, it had bothered him that Sam's unprecedented act of rebellion had involved Jamie—even though she'd done nothing to instigate the incident. He had wanted to keep whatever developed between himself and Jamie completely separate from his home life, and that wasn't made any easier by Sam's lingering obsession with her. He didn't know how to deal with his own fascination with Jamie—much less his five-year-old son's!

Turning away from the window, he finished his drink and set the glass aside. His gaze fell on the telephone sitting on a table beside the couch, illuminated by the dimmed light of the only lamp turned on in the shadowy den. Maybe he should call her. After all, she had brought Sam home safe to him. And he *had* been a bit short with her. He owed her another thank-you—and an apology.

He knew by her chilly tone that she'd already guessed who was calling. He didn't bother to identify himself before he said, "I suspect I wasn't as gracious to you this afternoon as I should have been."

"Why would you say that?" she asked too formally. "You thanked me for bringing Sam home and then you offered me a ride. You did everything that was expected of you."

He winced. "Jamie..."

"If you're calling to thank me again, please don't."

"I called because I want to talk to you. And because I know I behaved boorishly. All I can say is that I was badly shaken by Sam's disappearing act, and it made me forget my manners. It wasn't an excuse, but it's my only explanation."

"I understand that you were upset. I hope you've been able to reassure yourself it won't happen again."

"I had a long talk with Sam—and in case you're worried, I didn't yell at him. I merely pointed out that he scared the stuffing out of me, and I don't want him to even think about doing anything like that again."

"I'm sure he got your message."

"I certainly hope so."

"And Mrs. Brown?"

Hearing the uncertainty in her voice, he sighed wearily. "I didn't fire her."

"I'm glad."

"But I *did* make it clear that I want her to be prepared for any eventuality when it comes to Sam and Abbie."

"And what did she say?"

"That it had been a while since her son was that young and she'd almost forgotten how quickly they could get into mischief. She assured me she won't forget again."

"I doubt that she will. She looked genuinely worried about Sam this afternoon."

"She was," he conceded. "And she did call me the moment she realized he was missing."

"You might suggest to her that she try a slightly different approach with Sam. He complained to me that she talks down to him, and he doesn't like that."

"Yes, he finally told me the same thing. I'll talk to her about it tomorrow."

"Good. Was there anything else?"

"You're still annoyed with me," he said in resignation.

"Maybe just a little," she confessed, and he was pleased to hear a hint of ruefulness in her voice—as though she was prepared to forgive him, he thought hopefully. "You *were* kind of jerky to me."

Even after what had happened between them that afternoon, even suspecting that it wasn't a good idea, he wanted to see her again. Needed to see her again. And soon. "What can I do to make it up to you?"

"I don't know. I was pretty mad."

Relieved that she'd gotten past it enough to tease him, he responded in kind. "How about dinner? Would that be enough to make you forgive me?"

"Maybe..."

"And if I throw in a movie?"

"Add a large box of Gummi Bears and you're well on your way to being completely forgiven."

"I'll even spring for popcorn," he said, hoping his deep relief wasn't entirely evident in his voice.

"Nah. Movie popcorn's never tasted as good since they made it healthier."

"The new Tom Hanks film is playing in Carrolton," he suggested.

"Sounds good. When?"

"Friday?" It wasn't soon enough, but it would have to do.

"Friday. Oh, and Trev?"

"Yes?"

There was undisguised laughter in her voice when she replied, "Be prepared to grovel."

With that, she hung up the phone.

It was with some surprise that Trevor realized he was smiling as he replaced his own receiver. He hadn't expected this day to end with a smile. He could credit Jamie for that, of course.

Maybe he'd go to bed early tonight. He was tired, and not really in the mood for brooding.

He supposed he could thank Jamie for *that*, too.

TREVOR WAS GETTING READY for his date with Jamie Friday evening when the telephone rang. He'd already dropped the kids off at his parents' house; his mother was taking Sam, Abbie and Clay Davenport to the newest animated film that evening and then keeping them for a sleepover. He picked up the phone hoping nothing had gone wrong. As much as he had been looking forward to this evening, he would be deeply disappointed if something interfered. "Hello?"

"Hi, Trevor. It's Tara."

He felt his frown melt at the sound of his sister's voice. "Well, hi, yourself. How are you?"

"Miserable," she answered cheerfully. "I'm ready for this to be over."

"What's your doctor saying?"

"She keeps saying 'any day now.' She's been saying that for the past two weeks."

"How's Blake holding up?" Trevor asked, smiling as he mentioned his dashing, eccentric, private-investigator brother-in-law.

"He's a nervous wreck. As cool and patient as he can be in his work, imminent fatherhood has him rattled."

Trevor chuckled. "He'll be a great parent. You both will."

"I hope you're right. We have you, of course, to use as a role model."

Wincing, Trevor shook his head. "I'm not sure I qualify for that."

"Nonsense. You're doing a wonderful job raising Sam and Abbie. How are my little angels, by the way?"

"They're fine. Mother's taking them and Clay to see that new kids' movie this evening. I don't know whether or not Abbie will sit still long enough to watch it, but Mother seemed to think she would."

"Sam will like that. He always enjoys being with Clay. It's so cute the way he tries to emulate his older cousin."

"Yeah—and I'm relieved Clay's a decent kid for him to emulate."

"Clay's a sweetheart," Tara agreed fondly. "And Claire is adorable, isn't she? I talked to Emily this afternoon. She was delighted to announce that Claire's sleeping through the night, for the most part."

"Yes, well, Abbie's a year older than Claire and she still wakes up at least once most nights, so don't get your hopes too high for uninterrupted sleep for the next couple of years."

"How's Abbie doing with her walking?"

"She isn't." Trevor shook his head in resignation. "She's still just taking a few steps when she's holding on to things. Her pediatrician assures me there's nothing wrong with her. She just hasn't chosen to walk yet. She likes being carried."

"She'll decide soon that she'll have more fun when she can get around on her own two feet. And then you'll be complaining that you can't keep up with her."

"I'm sure you're right."

"So what are your plans for the evening? Going to sit around and enjoy the silence?"

"No, actually, I, uh, have plans."

"Plans?" He could almost see his sister's ears perk up. "Do you have a date?"

"Well, yes. Sort of." Since he was sure their mother would tell her, anyway, he added casually, "I'm taking Jamie Flaherty out for dinner and a movie."

"Jamie Flaherty? Really? I haven't seen her in years. Mother told me about her pulling Sam from the swimming pool a couple of weeks ago. I know you must be so grateful to her for that."

"Of course."

"I think this is great, Trevor. I'm glad you're getting out. You need to take some time for yourself."

"It's only dinner and a movie," he felt compelled to remind her, not wanting her to get any unfounded ideas.

"I bet Jamie has some fascinating stories to tell about her time in New York. I never knew her all that well, of course, since she was several years behind me in school, but I always thought she was incredibly talented. It was a shame Mrs. Lynch didn't showcase her as much as she should have in school plays. We all know why she didn't, of course, but it was so unfair."

Everyone in town had known about Jamie's unfortunate home life, of course, Trevor reflected. Her father had spent many a night drying out in the town jail and her mother was known as a vague, quiet woman with unfocused eyes and a fondness for cheap wine. Jamie had been well liked by her peers because of her outgoing nature and wicked sense of humor, but her parents had been a definite social disadvantage with the adults in town. Especially the other parents, who were reluctant for their sons to date her, or their daughters to spend too much time with her. As if her parents' drinking was a contagious disease that Jamie might carry, Trevor thought with a frown, looking back now with an adult's view of her youth.

How much had *he* been influenced by the whispers and rumors? Had his failure to ask her out then, even knowing there was a strong attraction between them, been due as much to unconscious snobbery as to wariness of their differences?

And wouldn't *that* have been hypocritical, coming from one of the wild McBrides?

Because the question made him uncomfortable, he abruptly changed the subject. "Have you heard from Trent lately?"

Tara's sigh carried clearly through the phone lines. "He called this morning. He wanted to know if—to use his words—I had 'dropped my load' yet."

Trevor chuckled. "That sounds exactly like the way he would have worded it. The kid's a fruitcake."

"I don't know, Trevor, I worry about him. He just sounds so cocky and reckless sometimes that I can't help being afraid he's going to get a rude awakening if he isn't careful. Does that make any sense to you?"

It made entirely too much sense, actually. Trevor had once been smug and cocky, himself, so certain his life was progressing exactly the way he had planned. So confident that nothing could go wrong. So stupidly blind to what had been going on right under his nose.

"Trent will be okay, Tara," he gruffly assured her. "You just take care of yourself, you hear? Your kid brothers can look after themselves."

Though she was barely a year older than Trevor and six years older than Trent, Tara had always taken her responsibility as the eldest too seriously. She'd always watched out for them and worried about them—which was one reason Trevor had never told her about his experience in Washington last year. She had grieved for him enough. She had her own life to enjoy now.

"I know you can both take care of yourselves," she

answered him affectionately. "It's just that I want you both to be happy."

"And Trent and I want the same for you, sis. It was great talking to you, but I'd better go now or I'll be late picking Jamie up."

"Tell her hello from me, will you?"

"Yes, I'll do that. And tell Blake to call as soon as the baby arrives so we can all come admire it."

"I hope that will be very soon," Tara said fervently.

"So do I. See you, Tara."

He hung up the phone and glanced at his watch.

It was time to pick up Jamie.

# 7

"SO THEN the director looked at me and said, 'Well, what are you waiting for? Get out there, Flaherty.'"

Trevor regarded Jamie intently over the rim of his coffee mug. "And what did you do?"

Curled on her couch beside him, her bare feet tucked beneath her, one arm propped on the back of the cushions, she grinned at him. "I went out there, of course. And I ad-libbed like crazy. And somehow, it worked. My reviews were better than I could have hoped for. Unfortunately, the critics weren't so kind to the rest of the show. It closed after two weeks."

"Was that when you decided to leave New York?"

"Heavens, no. That incident happened four years ago. I've been in three obscure plays and two soap operas since then."

"So why did you leave?"

"I've told you. My aunt Ellen called about the teaching position here and I decided to give it a try. I was actually working when she called me—a small, but interesting part in a critically well-received off-Broadway production. The public hasn't really discovered it yet, but I think it will happen soon."

Sometimes when Trevor looked at her, she felt as though he could look right into her head. It was those unnervingly intense blue eyes of his—they sometimes seemed to see too much. She wouldn't want him to guess that she'd come back partially because he was here. She had only recently admitted that to herself.

"So you just dropped everything in New York and came back here because you heard there was an opening for a drama teacher?" he asked, politely skeptical.

She lowered her eyelashes to conceal her expression—just in case he *could* see more than she wanted him to. "Yeah. Something like that."

He obviously didn't believe her, but he must have decided he had no right to pry any further. He took another sip of his coffee and set it aside. "I forgot to tell you that Tara called just before I left the house this evening. She said to tell you hello."

"How is she?"

"Ready for the baby to be born. They already know it's a girl. They're going to call her Alison."

"Pretty."

"Mom's beside herself, of course, at the thought of another grandchild. She does love being a grandma."

"You're lucky to have her. I know she's been a big help to you with the children."

"I don't know what I'd have done without her," he admitted. "She actually enjoys baby-sitting. She even asks me to let her keep the kids."

Jamie couldn't help comparing Trevor's family to her own. His could have come from a 1950s sitcom. Lawyer father, schoolteacher mother, three smart, well-behaved offspring. Sure, they were McBrides— but they'd been remarkably scandal-free in comparison to the other branches of the family, as far as Jamie knew. Had Trevor's wife not died in that car accident, he would probably still be living that Norman Rockwell life, himself.

Though the prospect of having her own children seemed remote at the moment, Jamie couldn't imagine *her* mother being a devoted grandparent. Lorena Flaherty spent her days in a blurry haze of booze and television. The only time she'd paid much attention to Jamie in the past few years was when Jamie had had a small, ten-week part on Lorena's favorite soap opera. During their usually stilted weekly phone calls, Lorena had pelted Jamie with questions about the other characters. Somewhat pitifully, she had seemed to truly believe the actors were the people they played—she'd even confused Jamie with her character a few times, chiding her for causing problems between a popular pair of lovers in the story.

She would have to give birth on the air to get her mother's attention, Jamie thought with long-resigned irony. And then she wondered what had triggered the thought. It wasn't as if she was planning to have children any time soon—if ever.

"Do you want more coffee?" she asked, nodding toward Trevor's empty cup.

"No. Actually, there's something I still have to do this evening."

"Oh?" She wasn't sure how to read his expression.

He nodded. "You told me to be prepared to grovel. I'm ready to do so now."

She'd almost forgotten their little spat earlier in the

week. "Perhaps you've noticed that I've forgiven you. Groveling isn't necessary at this point."

"You're sure?"

"Quite sure."

"I'm happy to hear that," he said, and pulled her toward him.

Her mouth only an inch or so from his, she murmured, "It was probably the case of Gummi Bears you brought when you picked me up this evening that did the trick."

He chuckled, his breath whisper-warm against her lips. "It was a toss-up between Gummi Bears and diamonds."

Cupping his face between her hands, she pulled him closer. "You made the right choice."

He couldn't know how much it had touched her to find him on her doorstep with the big box of candies in his hand. Diamonds could never have affected her the way the whimsical gesture and his slightly sheepish smile had.

She was crazy about his mouth, she thought as they dived into an eager kiss. His lower lip was full, his upper lip straight and firm. Two deep creases bracketed his smile—not dimples, exactly, but sexy hollows that begged to be explored with the tip of her tongue. Delicious.

They stretched the kiss out a very long time. When it ended, Jamie was sitting on Trevor's lap, his arms around her, hers locked around his neck. "Funny," she said. "I seem to keep ending up here."

"I'm not complaining."

"Neither am I." She rubbed her nose against his, as

amused as she was aroused. Even when he was teasing with her, he seemed so delightfully serious.

He caught her chin in his hand, pressing another kiss on her smiling lips. "I always get the feeling you're laughing at me," he murmured, displaying that unnerving mind-reading talent again.

"Only in the nicest way," she assured him, and kissed him again.

"What is it about me that amuses you so much?" he asked some time later.

Sliding a hand down his cheek, she laughed softly. "The way you're so serious all the time. The way you look at me sometimes as if you think I must come from another planet. The way your forehead creases when I say something that perplexes you. Shall I go on?"

"I think that's enough." His tone was dry.

"You're very seriously cute, Trevor McBride," she said, running her fingertips through his thick, dark blond hair. "You always have been."

"Cute?" His forehead wrinkled—exactly the way she'd just described. The way she found so endearing. "It's been a long time since anyone has called me cute."

She smiled. "Maybe you just haven't been listening."

Cupping his hand behind her head, he pulled her face toward him and traced her smile with the tip of his tongue. "I'm listening now."

She'd been waiting for so many years to get Trevor McBride's attention. Now that she had it, she intended to make the most of it—before he drifted away again. She covered his mouth with hers and kissed him exactly the way she had wanted to kiss him for so very long.

He moved with a speed that took her by surprise, shifting his weight until she was lying beneath him, pressed into the deep cushions of her jewel-tone couch. His mouth ravaged hers, tongues seeking, meeting, mating. Taking his cues from her, his hands raced over her with a boldness he hadn't shown before.

Jamie felt the fine tremors in his fingers, and she realized he was still holding back. He'd made it clear enough that he'd been living a monk's life for the past year. She didn't want to think he was with her now because she was convenient; she preferred to think of herself as the woman who had drawn him out of his self-imposed exile.

He shifted restlessly, and she felt the hardness pressing against her thigh. Whatever the barriers that had come between them in the past, they were together now and he wanted her. She couldn't guess how long it would last, or even if they would ever be together again after tonight. But she had no intention of missing this one chance to fulfill a fifteen-year-old fantasy.

She slid her hands down his back, relishing the ripple of muscle beneath his clothing. He was still exploring her mouth so thoroughly she was sure he had memorized every centimeter. She knew she would never forget the taste or the texture of his.

She felt his right hand sliding upward from her hip to her rib cage—suddenly tentative, as if he wasn't quite sure of her reaction. She arched into his touch, mutely letting him know her reaction was decidedly positive. She almost felt the surge of heat rush through him when his hand closed finally over her left breast.

He wanted her, she thought again, every nerve ending vibrating with reciprocal excitement.

Trevor slid his mouth from her lips to her jaw, moved to the shallow indention in her chin, then buried his face in her throat to measure the pulse beating so rapidly in the hollow there. She shifted to accommodate him, sliding her fingers into his hair, lifting herself more firmly into his embrace.

A sudden shrill buzzing pierced the intimate silence between them, causing Jamie to gasp in surprise and Trevor to lift his head with a start. She was so disoriented that it took her a moment to identify the sound as a cellular telephone. By that time, Trevor had already pulled a flip-phone the size of a deck of playing cards out of his pocket. Giving her a look of apology, he straightened, opened the phone and lifted it to his ear. His voice was admirably composed when he said, "Hello?"

Resigned to the inevitable, Jamie wriggled into an upright position, straightened her clothes and smoothed her hair. "I hope it wasn't a crisis," she said when Trevor completed the brief call and slid the phone back into his pocket.

"Not a crisis, but I have to go," he said, regret in his voice. "Abbie's running a fever and she keeps crying for me. Mother tried to handle it, but she doesn't think Abbie's going to settle down unless I'm there."

"Then you should go. Are you going to take her to the emergency room?" The word *fever* had already made Jamie nervous; she wondered how Trevor could sound so calm about it.

With just a hint of a smile, he shook his head. "It's just a cold. She's been coming down with it for a couple of days. She seemed to be feeling better this morning, so I thought we'd be okay, but apparently she's feeling worse again."

"Poor baby. I hate to think of her crying for you."

He squeezed her hand. "I'm sorry our evening is ending so abruptly."

"So am I," she said, but she smiled to show that she understood. "I had a great time, Trev."

"So did I." He stood, and she rose to follow him to the door. He paused with one hand on the doorknob, his gaze searching her face. "Jamie—it isn't easy for a single father to find time for a personal life."

"I'm sure it isn't."

"I work long hours and I don't want to spend a lot of time away from the kids when I'm not at the office."

"They need you," Jamie agreed simply, admiring his dedication to his children.

He nodded. "My mother's been trying to convince me that one evening a week isn't too much to take for myself. And she likes having that time to bond with her grandchildren. To be honest, I still feel guilty about taking any time at all away from them, but I've about reached the conclusion that she's right. I need some time for myself."

She wasn't sure where, exactly, he was leading with this, but she nodded. "Of course you do."

His grimace let her know that he wasn't satisfied with the way his words were coming out. "I'm trying to say that I want to see you again."

She smiled. "I'd like that, too."

"Next Friday?"

"I have no plans for next Friday."

He leaned over to plant a quick, firm kiss against her lips. "You do now. I'll call."

"Do that. I hope Abbie feels better soon."

"Thanks. G'night, Jamie."

"Good night, Trev." She watched him walk to his car, but closed the door before she could be tempted to watch him drive out of sight.

With a bemused sigh, she turned away from the door as the sound of his car engine faded into silence. Her gaze fell on the couch, where the throw pillows, scattered on the floor and scrunched at one end, reminded her of exactly what his phone call had interrupted. She sighed again, this time in wistfulness.

He wanted to see her again.

She spared a fleeting thought for her old rule—no men with children. Tonight was a prime example why she'd made that rule in the first place. She'd always considered herself too selfish to share a man's time with his kids, especially since she knew she would always come second in his priorities. Which was the way it should be, of course—she certainly couldn't be interested in a man who put his children second.

Shaking her head at her own inconsistencies where

Trevor McBride was involved, she crossed the room to straighten the pillows. She would see Trevor again in a week, she thought. Now all she had to do was figure out how to entertain herself in the meantime.

ABBIE'S TOO-WARM little face was buried in the curve of Trevor's throat, her sleep-limp body curled snugly into his arms. She'd dropped off almost as soon as he'd picked her up, having fought sleep as long as she could. He sat in his mother's dimly lit kitchen, a cup of herbal tea in front of him, while Bobbie sipped her own tea on the other side of the table. The house was quiet, with everyone else having gone to bed before Abbie's fretful outburst.

"I'm sorry I had to cut your evening short," Bobbie said. "I didn't know what else to do with her. She refused to let me comfort her. She wanted her daddy."

"It's only because she doesn't feel well."

"I didn't take it personally," Bobbie assured him. "I just regretted having to spoil your evening with Jamie."

Trevor made a production of straightening Abbie's nightgown. "No problem. We were only having coffee and talking."

"Mmm." Her tone made him feel like a teenager whose protestations of innocence weren't quite ringing true. "You like Jamie, don't you?"

Now she was talking to him as if he were that same teenager. He gave her a look over his daughter's head. "Yeah, Mom, I like her. I thought I would ask Wade to ask Emily to ask Jamie if she likes me, too."

She frowned at him. "There's no need for sarcasm."

"Well, what do you expect? I'm thirty-one, and you're quizzing me as if I were sixteen."

"I wasn't trying to pry. I just think it's nice that you're getting out. You've been so isolated and withdrawn since you moved back to Honoria. It's time for you to start living again."

"I've hardly stopped living since I moved back. I've been kind of busy. Starting almost from scratch in private practice, learning Dad's business, taking care of the kids..."

"But you haven't had much fun," Bobbie broke in. "I think if anyone can bring plain old fun back into your life, it's Jamie Flaherty. I'll admit she's a little eccentric—one could hardly expect otherwise considering her raising—but I've always liked her. Even when she went through her rebellious stage—that would have been after you left for college, I suppose—I knew she was really a nice girl with a good head on her shoulders. I wasn't at all surprised when Ellen told me Jamie was coming back from New York to take the drama position. I knew she'd only moved there to get away from home. Playacting was always her way of escaping, and she was good at it."

"I've never seen her act," Trevor admitted, "but I would imagine that she's very good at it." He suspected that Jamie was good at anything she tried—and a few of those things he was becoming very impatient to find out for himself.

"You are going to see her again, aren't you?"

"Next weekend. But, Mom, Jamie and I are just

friends, okay? Don't start making more out of it than that."

"But, Trevor..."

"I mean it, Mom. Jamie and I aren't a couple. I don't want you getting carried away."

"But I'm sure Melanie would have wanted you to—"

"And *don't* bring Melanie into this!" Roused by Trevor's sharp tone, Abbie stirred and fretted. He already regretted his outburst—for the baby's sake, and for his mother's. Rocking Abbie back to sleep, he spoke more quietly. "I'm sorry, Mom."

She didn't look offended. In fact, he thought he saw sympathetic understanding in her eyes. "Someday," she said, "when you're ready, you'll talk to me about what happened between you and Melanie. In the meantime, just know that I'm here, all right? I won't pry into your business, I won't interfere between you and Jamie, and I'll gladly watch the children for you whenever you need me to. I only want you to be happy again, Trevor."

Feeling somewhat akin to a slug now, Trevor managed a faint apologetic smile. "I know. It's all you've ever wanted for any of us."

She nodded, then glanced at the clock on the stove. "It's getting very late."

"You must be tired. Why don't you turn in? I'll take Abbie home and put her to bed, then I'll come back tomorrow to get Sam."

"There's no need for you to do that. Abbie's crib is already set up in your old bedroom, and I just put fresh sheets on the bed this morning. Sam and Clay are sound asleep in Trent's room, and your father is snoring away in ours. You might as well sleep over and have breakfast with us in the morning."

"I—"

"It's settled, then." Bobbie stood. "I have a couple of new toothbrushes around here somewhere. I'll put one in your bathroom. There's still a bathrobe hanging in your closet, and an extra..."

"I know where everything is, Mom. But I—"

"Don't argue. It isn't as if you have any reason to go home."

He knew she hadn't meant it the way it had sounded, but her words left him feeling hollow, anyway. His mother was right, he thought as he changed Abbie's diaper and tucked her into her crib a few minutes later. There really wasn't any reason for him to go home.

JAMIE HAD JUST HUNG UP her phone late Wednesday morning when it rang again. Still thinking about the last call, she raised the receiver to her ear and said a bit absently, "Hello?"

"Hi."

The single syllable was enough to claim her full attention. "Hi, Trev. How's Abbie?"

"Much better, thanks. She felt pretty lousy all weekend, but by yesterday she was completely back to normal."

"I'm happy to hear that."

"Have you had lunch yet?"

"No." She glanced at her watch, noting that it was almost noon.

"I've got an hour and a half before my next appointment. How about if I pick up some takeout and bring it to your place?"

"Is this another impulsive action?" she asked, delighted.

"I guess you're corrupting me."

She laughed softly. "I haven't even gotten started."

"Should I take that as a threat—or a promise?"

"Whichever you like."

"I'll see you in fifteen minutes."

Jamie hung up the phone again, then jumped to her feet. Maybe she should put on a little makeup or something, she thought, hurrying toward the bedroom.

It was almost exactly fifteen minutes later when Trevor rang the doorbell. She threw the door open with a smile. "Hi."

Carrying a couple of aromatic paper bags, Trevor nodded. "Hi, yourself."

"Here, let me take one of those. We can eat in the kitchen."

He followed close on her heels as she led the way. "I'm glad you were free," he said.

Setting the bag on the table, she shrugged ruefully. "I seem to have a lot more free time than I'm used to these days."

"Sounds as though you're already getting tired of small-town life."

She lifted an eyebrow in response to something she heard in his voice. He seemed to be expecting her to agree with him. "Not really," she said. "It's just taking me a while to figure out what to do with my time this summer. Actually, something just came up that sounds interesting."

"Oh?" He dug into a bag and pulled out a paper-wrapped sandwich, his voice casual. "What's that?"

"Earlene Smithee called earlier this morning. She's been contemplating starting a community theater group and she wanted to know if I would be interested in sharing my expertise. She has several acquaintances who want to get involved, but they don't know how."

"Community theater?" He looked at her curiously then. "Would you really be interested in getting into something like that?"

"Why not? It might be fun."

"Hmm. And it might be a bunch of aging beauty pageant queens like Earlene who just want a chance to get back in the spotlight."

"You've just pretty well described most community theater groups," she informed him with a chuckle. "They're generally made up of volunteers who always secretly dreamed of acting, but never quite had the courage to pursue it."

"Or the talent," he suggested, thinking of Earlene.

She shrugged. "That, too, of course. But the right director can put even limited talent to use with the right script and enough hard work."

"The right director meaning you?"

"I wouldn't mind directing a play for them. It wouldn't be that much different than working with my students."

"Except that your students are required to do what you tell them. Earlene's never been very good at following directions. And what if April Penny decides she wants to join? You know she and Earlene hate each other. Could you handle it if they got into a hair-pulling fight over a part?"

"You really do underestimate me, don't you? Must I remind you I've worked in New York? I've seen soap opera starlets try to claw each other's eyes out because one was certain the other was trying to up-stage her. I've heard them call each other names that would turn your hair white. April and Earlene are amateurs when it comes to true divahood."

"'Divahood'?" Trevor repeated the phrase with a quizzical smile. "Is that what it's called?"

"That's what I call it."

"And do you consider yourself a diva?"

She laughed. "I'm afraid I never qualified. Only the big stars—soap, stage or film—can be considered true divas. I was just that nice young character actor with the big eyes and the funny accent."

"Is that how you saw yourself?"

"That's how the casting people saw me."

She pulled two plates out of a cabinet and set them on the table, smiling to show him that she had long since learned to accept her fate. She might have worked harder, longer, more fiercely, but the chances of her ever becoming a big star had been slim. She could have made a steady, even generous, income in New York, or in Los Angeles, but she'd finally real-ized that there was an emptiness inside her that could only be filled by coming back here and dealing once and for all with her past.

Trevor McBride had been very much a part of that past, whether he was aware of it or not.

"So you're going to start a community theater." He still seemed to find that hard to believe.

"Sounds like it. Want to join? I can see you wearing a torn T-shirt and yelling, 'Stella!'"

He gave her a look that made her giggle. "I don't think so."

"No hidden desires to be onstage, pretending to be someone else? No longing to hear the thunder of applause in your ears?"

"No. I'm quite content to sit quietly in the audience. I'll buy a ticket for your production, Jamie—even if Earlene Smithee plays the ingenue—but I won't do any acting."

"Pity," she said with an exaggerated sigh, reaching up to trail her fingertips along his firm jawline. "I have a feeling that gorgeous, sexy leading men will be in short supply around here."

She was satisfied to see a faint color tinge his skin. He reached up to catch her hand. "You're trying to embarrass me again, aren't you?"

"And succeeding, apparently."

He gave a quick, unexpected tug on her wrist that brought her up against him. "What does it take to make *you* blush, Jamie Flaherty?"

"I don't know," she murmured. "But you're welcome to try."

"I've always been one to enjoy a challenge," he said against her lips. And then smothered her taunting reply with his mouth.

# 8

WHATEVER THEY'D been talking about completely left Jamie's mind. The lunch Trevor had brought with him no longer held her interest. She was ravenous—but not for sandwiches.

He slid his hands down her back, slowly, pressing her more closely against him. It didn't take her long to realize she wasn't the only one with needs more urgent than food.

She slid her arms around his neck and parted her lips for him, inviting him to deepen the kiss—which he did, thoroughly. The cropped, olive-green top she wore with her khaki cargo shorts had ridden up when she lifted her arms, baring an expanse of skin at her midriff. Trevor took full advantage of the opportunity to explore. His palms were deliciously warm against the skin of her back. She could only imagine how good they would feel on the rest of her.

"Jamie," he muttered against her lips, his voice rough. "We'd better stop this if we're going to eat lunch."

"Stop what?" She moved very slightly as she spoke, the lightest brush of her breasts against his chest.

He groaned. "That."

She nipped at his chin, savoring the spicy taste of

him, enjoying the quiver of reaction that ran through him. "This?"

His hands gripped her hips, as if he intended to push her away. Instead, he pulled her closer, bringing her more snugly against him. "You're playing with fire, Jamie."

"Are you warning me that I might get burned?"

"Maybe I'm more concerned that you'll burn *me*," he muttered, his lips moving over the soft skin behind her ear.

Her heart was beating so hard now that she felt almost as though she should raise her voice to be heard above it. And yet her words came out as little more than a husky whisper. "Maybe we'll burn together."

He shifted, and she found herself lifted against his chest, her feet dangling two inches above the floor. She looked into his face and saw that the humor was gone. His eyes glittered, and his cheekbones seemed suddenly more prominent, evidence of the tension that gripped him. "I can't joke about this."

Holding his gaze with her own, she said absolutely seriously, "What makes you think I'm joking?"

The moment seemed to last a very long time. Breaths were held. Limbs quivered. And then Trevor lowered her slowly to her feet, letting her slide down him, and covered her mouth with a kiss so perfect, so special that it brought a lump to her throat.

She hadn't intended to give him her heart. It was the only part of herself she had planned to hold back. But damn if he hadn't slipped through her defenses and stolen it, anyway.

She'd been infatuated with Trevor McBride when

she was fifteen. A lot of things had changed since then, but her feelings for Trevor felt very much the same. Maybe they were even more serious now that she was mature enough to understand how very much was at stake.

She'd had so little to offer him then. He'd been the golden boy—with so much ahead of him, so little lacking in his life. But things were different now. She sensed a deep need in him—an aching hole—and she thought she just might have what he needed now. At least for a while.

The tender kiss finally ended. Jamie reached up to cup his face between her hands. She smiled tenderly when she asked, "What do you want now? Sandwiches or sex?"

He gave a quick, startled laugh, his grim expression suddenly easing. "Damn it, Jamie."

She lifted an eyebrow. "Was that an answer or just an expletive?"

Though her hands still rested on his face, he shook his head. "How can you look so completely serious when you say things like that?"

"Because I *was* completely serious," she said, secretly pleased that she'd coaxed even a little laugh from him. He needed laughter as much—if not more—than he needed physical release.

"I came here today to have lunch with you. I wasn't expecting anything else."

"Neither was I," she said. "And—in case you get the wrong idea—sex isn't something I indulge in very often. In fact, I haven't indulged in quite a while. But the offer still stands."

"You don't know how much I want to take you up on it," he almost groaned. "But I think we'd better eat our sandwiches today. I have to be back at the office for a one-thirty meeting."

"Cola or iced tea?" she asked without a pause.

He blinked, then mentally caught up. "Uh, cola's fine."

Dropping her hands to her side, she moved toward the refrigerator. No way would she let him see the extent of her disappointment—or the faint relief that they hadn't yet complicated their relationship to a point where her life would never quite be the same.

"BOY, you've been growling like a coon dog with a thorn in its paw all afternoon. What in blazes is the matter with you?"

Trevor looked over the rim of his reading glasses with a repressive frown. "You can drop the simple-country-lawyer routine, Dad. It's just us here now, and I'm not going to fall for it."

Sitting on the other side of Trevor's desk, his feet propped up and crossed at the ankles, Caleb chuckled. "Even a simple country lawyer could tell that you're in a lousy mood. What's wrong?"

Trevor removed the glasses and set them aside. "Nothing."

Caleb looked blatantly disbelieving.

"Okay," Trevor conceded. "This Foster case is a major headache. I hate seeing a marriage end this unpleasantly, especially when there are kids caught in the middle."

Amusement fading, Caleb nodded. "It has gotten

ugly, hasn't it? You'd think Clark and Valerie would make an effort to keep the boys from hearing some of their crap. But when they start fighting, they don't seem to care who hears them."

"I couldn't believe Valerie brought the younger boy with her for that confrontation this afternoon." Trevor's voice was hard as he thought about his client's irresponsible action. "He might be only four, but the kid isn't deaf or stupid. He heard the things his parents were saying to each other. After a few minutes, I asked Marie to come take the boy to her office. She kept him busy drawing pictures and making copies of them on the copier."

"I bet you had a few things to say to your client when the boy was out of hearing."

"Actually, I did. And to give him credit, Clark's attorney agreed with every word I said."

"Bill Walker, isn't it? I know you haven't met him under ideal circumstances, but he's a good man. I've faced him several times in court, but I've always respected him, even when I disagreed with him."

"He seemed all right, even if he and Clark are being unreasonable about several issues in the divorce."

"He's just doing his best for his client, son, the way you will for yours. Divorces aren't pretty, and getting involved in them is never fun. Many a time I've left meetings like the one you had this afternoon feeling as if I needed a shower. But you should know by now that divorces and bankruptcies are a big part of small-town practice. It can't all be writing wills and working up small-business contracts."

"I knew what I was getting into. This afternoon was just particularly unpleasant."

"So you haven't changed your mind about taking over the practice when I retire in a couple of years? You still want to spend the rest of your career doing this?"

"As opposed to going back to Washington, you mean? Trust me, Dad, that catfight this afternoon didn't hold a candle to what goes on in D.C. I haven't changed my mind. I just don't like seeing kids get hurt."

"I know. So you keep doing all you can to protect them."

"I'll try."

Studying his son over steepled fingers, Caleb asked, "Anything else bothering you?"

"No, that's pretty much it." Trevor looked at the papers on his desk as he spoke, hoping his father would take his words at face value.

Known for his tact—as opposed to his wife, who was notorious for her lack of it—Caleb didn't push, except to ask, "Anything else you want to talk about?"

"Not just now."

His father nodded and stood. "Then I'll clear out so you can finish up and get home to your kids. You let me know if there's anything I can do for you—or if you just want to talk about anything."

"Thanks, Dad."

Trevor frowned as he watched his father rise slowly from his seat. Since when had Caleb moved so stiffly? So awkwardly? Like an old man, he thought, displeased with the comparison. Had he been so caught up in his own troubles that he hadn't realized how quickly his parents were aging? Was there anything else he was missing? "Dad? You okay?"

Absently rubbing his chest, Caleb made a face. "Fine. Been having some heartburn trouble lately. Getting old ain't fun, boy."

"Have you seen anyone about it?"

"Bobbie's been nagging at me to get a physical. I'll get around to it shortly."

"Do that."

It was obvious, Trevor thought after Caleb left his office, that he hadn't been doing a very good job lately hiding his emotional turmoil from his parents. At first, he'd been struggling with the repercussions of Melanie's death and the things he'd found out afterward. Now he was trying to deal with his overwhelming attraction to Jamie. Both of his parents had expressed concern about him.

He'd been honest with his father. He hadn't changed his mind about settling here, raising his children here, eventually taking over the McBride law firm. He was generally satisfied with his career, and accepted that every job came with its highs and lows. Divorces were an ugly but unavoidable part of life, and he was prepared to do his best to make the ones he handled as smooth and equitable as possible.

He supposed he'd been particularly affected today because he had looked at Valerie and Clark's unhappy little boy and had pictured Sam. Had things been different—had Melanie not died in that traffic accident on a busy Washington, D.C., intersection after leaving a lunchtime tryst with one of her lovers—they could have been the ones facing each other across a divorce table, viciously airing their private pain and fighting for custody of their children.

The thought made him cringe. Relief that he and his kids had been spared those scenes was followed by an immediate wave of guilt that his reprieve had come at such a terrible price for Melanie.

It was a wearily familiar battle, one he usually fought alone in the middle of the night with a single shot of bourbon as his only emotional support. There was no one he could talk to, no one he wanted to burden with the painful revelations he had struggled with for so long. For his children's sake, for Melanie's memory, and maybe for his own pride, he couldn't talk about it. Not yet. Maybe not ever.

A woman's voice came from the speaker on his desk phone, bringing him abruptly back to the present. "Trevor?"

Trevor cleared his throat. "Yes, Marie?"

"I'm leaving now. Is there anything else you need before I go?"

"No, I'm about to head home, myself. See you tomorrow."

He gathered the paperwork scattered over his desk and stuffed it into a folder, then saved and exited the file on his computer screen. His thoughts had already left the office, racing to the evening ahead of him. He'd run out of coffee that morning and was almost out of milk; he would have to stop by the store on the way home. Sarah had promised to put a pot roast and vegetables in the oven for him, so all he would have to do was serve the kids, bathe them, read them a couple of stories and tuck them into bed. He would then have the remainder of the evening to himself— to remember, to brood, to regret.

Maybe he'd give Jamie a call after the kids were in bed. They'd started a conversation over lunch about the community theater, but he'd had to cut it short to get back to the office. Maybe they could discuss it further later. And maybe, sometime during their discussion about the future of art in Honoria, he could figure out why the *hell* he had turned down what she had offered instead of lunch today.

It was something he was beginning to think he needed very badly.

"I STILL DON'T UNDERSTAND why we can't do *Phantom of the Opera.*" Earlene Smithee, who, twenty years earlier, had served a year as Miss Junior Honoria, spoke plaintively on the following Sunday afternoon. "I've always really identified with Christine, you know?"

Jamie didn't laugh—but it wasn't easy. Earlene was long past playing ingenue roles, and as far as her play suggestion... "I really don't think that's a possibility, Earlene. We'd probably better stick with something simpler for our first production."

Earlene sighed, but conceded, "You're the expert."

Jamie didn't feel particularly like an expert—especially when it came to organizing a community theater from scratch—but she hid her uncertainty behind a confident smile. "I'll bring several plays to our next meeting. If anyone else has any recommendations, please feel free to bring them along."

The seven aspiring actors and techies Earlene had assembled for the first organizational meeting of the Honoria Community Theater nodded eagerly, watching Jamie as if she was their wise guru and they her faithful followers. She knew that would wear off when they'd spent more time together, but she was rather enjoying the treatment now.

"Okay, so I'll see everyone here next week. And feel free to bring friends. It takes a number of volunteers to put on a quality production."

The meeting adjourned and everyone began to file out of the community room of the Honoria Methodist Church. Several people stopped to speak to Jamie on the way out, sharing their experiences from high-school plays and church pageants, a rather sheepish lust for applause glimmering in their eyes.

"You were wonderful in *Private Lives*," a young housewife—Jamie thought her name was Sherry—said with shy admiration. Sherry was about her own age, but tended to speak to Jamie with a reverence usually reserved for aging heroes. "It's my favorite soap—and I saw every one of the episodes you were in."

"Thank you. I enjoyed playing that part."

"How could you give it all up to move back to Honoria?" Sherry asked in open bewilderment. "I've only lived here for a couple of years and sometimes I get so bored I could scream."

Jamie chuckled. "I guess you could say I got homesick. Besides, I was ready for a change. Even constant activity can become tedious after a while."

"I could use a little excitement, myself."

"You should definitely audition for a part in whatever play we choose," Jamie encouraged, guessing that Sherry would perform very well. "It would certainly be a new challenge for you."

"I'll do that. Thanks."

Susan Schedler approached Jamie when the others had departed. Jamie was gathering the notes she'd made during the meeting; she looked up with a smile when her pregnant friend waddled closer.

Susan looked around to make sure the others were gone, then burst into giggles. *"Phantom of the Opera?"*

Jamie grinned. "Don't get me started. It was all I could do not to laugh in poor Earlene's face."

"She's probably going to audition for the youngest part in whatever play you select, you know. And she isn't going to like it when you cast her as an aging matron or someone's mother."

"I'll worry about that when I'm casting parts."

"You're sure you want to get involved with this? A bunch of rank amateurs with dreams of local stardom?"

Wrinkling her nose, Jamie replied, "It just might be fun. And, besides, I need something productive to do."

"Getting bored, are you?"

"Maybe a little," Jamie admitted, though she knew it wasn't boredom, exactly. More of a dissatisfaction—an awareness that something was still lacking in her life. Something that her one-night-a-week dates with Trevor weren't quite compensating for.

"I find that hard to believe, considering how often

the town's most eligible lawyer comes calling on you."

Jamie went still, wondering for a moment if her friend had just read her mind. "I beg your pardon?"

Susan's smile was mischievous. "Surely you haven't forgotten how efficient the Honoria rumor mill is."

Jamie groaned. "Don't tell me..."

"Oh, yes. Folks have been talking about you and Trevor McBride. They're saying you've been out with him on several Friday evenings, including the most recent one. *And* that his car was spotted at your house in the middle of a weekday."

"We had lunch. He brought takeout," Jamie muttered.

"Mmm. And what did you have for dessert?"

"Conversation," Jamie answered repressively. And their date Friday had ended when, after several long, arousing kisses, Trevor had rather abruptly departed, leaving her quivering with pent-up desire.

She was beginning to wonder if she shouldn't just drag him into her bedroom and attack him, putting an end to the anticipation.

"Well?" Susan demanded.

"Well, what?"

"What's going on?"

"Nothing much. Trevor and I are just friends." *For now, at least.*

"Two lonely singles sharing dinner and conversation?"

Jamie stuffed her notes into her oversize tote bag. "Something like that."

"Want to know the local odds for and against the two of you getting married?"

"No."

Susan laughed. "Let's just say it's evenly divided."

Jamie slung the strap of her tote over her shoulder. This, she thought, was exactly why she and Trevor had made a point of being discreet about their dates, choosing restaurants and movie theaters in different towns. Apparently, their efforts had been a waste of time.

"*Everyone* is talking about us?" she asked.

"Everyone," Susan replied cheerfully. "Martha Godwin says she thinks Trevor will be a good influence on you. She says he might even convince you to tone down your hair color. She thinks you'll be a pretty good stepmom, with Bobbie to guide you, of course. Nellie Hankins is appalled that anyone would even consider getting involved with a McBride, but she supposes you're as good a match as any for them, considering you're an actress, and everyone knows what kind of life *they* live."

Jamie didn't know whether to cringe or laugh at Susan's wicked summation of the local gossip. "With friends like you..."

"I just thought you'd want to know what's being said. But, if it makes you feel any better, most folks around here have gotten to really like you since you've moved back, and they think you and Trevor make a nice couple. I tend to agree with that point of view, by the way."

Shaking her head, Jamie accompanied Susan out of the church and into the parking lot. "Something tells me Trevor's going to hate this. He seems to have an especially strong aversion to gossip."

"Can you blame him? He's a McBride."

"Yes, I know. But they have all been model citizens lately. Lucas has been cleared of all suspicion of murder, Savannah's a respectably married mother, as are Emily and Tara. Trent's an air force officer and Trevor's a devoted father and a respected attorney. The old scandals have surely faded in most people's memories."

"Old habits die hard around here. Folks still talk about Trevor's great-grandfather, who was suspected of running a gang of horse thieves. And the gossips do hate losing their favorite targets. They'll keep watching the McBrides and hoping for some juicy new development. They're thinking you might be just that."

Though she knew Susan was only trying to be helpful by sharing what was being said about her, Jamie didn't like what she was hearing. Trevor was skittish enough about their developing relationship as it was. If he heard that she was the catalyst for renewed gossip about him, he was likely to bolt. And she wasn't ready for that just yet.

JAMIE DREW a deep breath when the doorbell rang just after noon on Tuesday. A quick check in a wall mirror let her know that her hair was reasonably tidy, and her deep-scooped white T-shirt was neatly tucked into her short khaki skirt. Her legs were bare except for the leather sandals that revealed her silver-painted toenails. Trying to look as if she'd given hardly any thought at all to her appearance, she flung open the door. "Hi, Trev."

"Hi." He stepped inside, closing the door behind him. "You look very nice."

"Thanks. I'm glad you were free for lunch today. When I called to invite you, I half expected you to be too busy."

"Actually, it's a slow day at the office. Mom and Dad left this morning to meet their new granddaughter, and my next appointment isn't until three o'clock. Your invitation was a nice surprise."

She was delighted to hear that—and to discover that he didn't have to hurry back. "How is the new grandchild?" she asked, trying to keep her tone casual.

"I talked to Blake this morning, when Alison was only five hours old. According to him, his daughter is the most beautiful and talented child ever born. He's wrong, of course, since my own children already hold that distinction, but I allowed him to hang on to his illusions."

"That was very generous of you."

"I thought so." And then he changed the subject. "Something smells good."

"I just took some rolls out of the oven. It's so warm out today, I thought we'd have a light lunch. Chicken salad, fruit and wheat rolls."

"Sounds good. Much better than the burger I was expecting."

"Then let's eat. Everything's ready. Feel free to take off the jacket and tie, if you like. I don't run a formal dining room."

She didn't wait to see if he followed her teasing suggestion, but turned to walk into the kitchen. He joined her only moments later. She had just retrieved a pitcher of iced tea from the refrigerator, and she deliberately tightened her grip to keep from dropping it when she looked at him. Trevor had shed his jacket and tie, had unfastened the top button of his white shirt and rolled the sleeves up on his forearms. She didn't know whether he'd run a hand through his hair, or whether it had fallen onto his forehead when he'd removed his tie, but it looked sexily tousled now.

The guy was gorgeous, she thought with a silent, wistful sigh. It was all she could do not to wrap herself around him right there in her kitchen. "Sweetened or unsweetened?" she asked, indicating the tea pitcher in her hands.

Trevor gave her a look that made her stomach muscles flutter. "I like my tea sweet."

Feeling bold again, she sauntered to the table, set the pitcher down and asked in a drawl, "And how do you like your women?"

"Spicy," he answered without hesitation.

Delighted, she ran her fingertips down his cheek as she moved past him to her chair. "I think I *am* corrupting you, Trev."

"You haven't heard me complaining, have you?"

"Not yet." She wondered what he'd do when he heard that the local scandalmongers were placing bets on their future.

During lunch, she told him about the community theater meeting, leaving out Susan's revelations afterward, of course. Trevor chuckled when she mentioned Earlene's grandiose suggestions, then nodded thoughtfully when she mentioned the three plays she planned to recommend at the next meeting.

"I think you're right to stick with lightweight comedies for now," he said. "You should have better public response."

"That's what I thought. People are less likely to be overly critical when they're laughing—which means, of course, that I'll have to make sure they *do* laugh."

"Sounds like a lot of work. And a big commitment on everyone's part—especially yours. Sure you want to be tied down to that?"

She shrugged. "I'm not planning to leave town any time soon. And I like being active in the community."

"I hope it goes well for you."

"Thanks. You're sure I can't talk you into auditioning for a part?"

"I would rather be tied up and beaten with banana peels," he said with blunt humor.

She looked at him from beneath her lashes. "Really? I didn't know you were into that sort of thing, but I'm sure it can be arranged."

He set his tea glass on the table with a thump. "Behave yourself," he ordered gruffly, visibly reacting to her sizzling look and sultry voice.

She laughed and turned her attention back to her lunch.

By the time their plates were emptied, Jamie was pleased to note that Trevor looked more relaxed than usual. His blue eyes were unshadowed, and a faint smile softened his sexy mouth. Gossip or not, she had come to the conclusion that she was good for him. Now all she had to do was to convince Trevor.

She stood and gathered their dishes, arranging them efficiently in the dishwasher. "What would you like for dessert?"

She hadn't realized that Trevor had risen from his seat until she heard his voice directly behind her. "You," he said, his arms sliding around her waist.

Her skin warming, she leaned back against him, laying her hands on his crossed wrists. "Most people want something sweet for dessert."

"I prefer spicy." He nuzzled the back of her neck, his lips tasting the sensitive skin at her nape.

Her eyelids felt suddenly heavy. "So do I, actually."

"That doesn't surprise me." His right hand slid upward from her waist, pausing just an inch below her breast. She knew he could feel her heart pounding frantically against her ribs, but she made no effort to hide her reactions from him. If he didn't know by now that she wanted him, he hadn't been paying very close attention.

He shifted an inch closer, so that he was pressed more tightly to her, proving that she wasn't the only one with wants. She moved lightly against him, drawing a husky sound from deep in his chest. Dipping his head lower, he nipped at a patch of shoulder revealed by her deeply cut T-shirt. "Jamie?"

Her eyes were almost closed. She tilted her head and lifted her shoulder to give him better access. "Mmm?"

"I have a couple of hours before I have to be back at the office."

She turned in his arms, placing her hands on his shoulders and searching his face. "And you want to spend those hours with me?"

"I want to spend those hours making love to you," he clarified.

She didn't know what had changed since Friday night, when he'd abruptly pulled away from her and almost run from her house—just as he had the Friday before that. She wasn't sure what had changed his mind, or why it had happened now. But she wasn't going to try to talk him out of it. "I can't think of a better way to spend a couple of hours."

The skin around his mouth had grown taut during her brief hesitation. Her words made him relax. "Neither can I."

She pushed lightly against him, forcing him to take a step back, and then she took his hand. Without a word, she moved toward the kitchen doorway.

Without a word, he followed.

# 9

JAMIE HAD CLOSED the drapes in her bedroom so that the room was dark, except for the small, dimmed lamp on the nightstand. Her ruffled comforter was turned back invitingly, revealing fresh, soft sheets. There was no doubt that the scene had been set in advance.

Trevor turned to her with a quizzical smile. She returned it with a somewhat smug smile of her own. "You can't blame a girl for hoping," she said, kicking off her shoes.

He laughed, then grabbed her around the waist and tumbled her onto the bed. "You," he said, landing on top of her, "are incorrigible."

Maybe. But she had made him laugh. And that was something she'd bet few other woman had been able to offer him lately. Eager to taste his smile, she reached up to pull his mouth down to hers.

His laughter evaporated in a flash of fire. Gathering her into his arms, he swept her into the heat with him.

Her short skirt had ridden high on her thighs and Trevor didn't hesitate to explore the expanse of skin revealed beneath it. He slid his palm slowly from her knee to the bunched hem, then slipped beneath it.

Catching her breath, Jamie fumbled with his shirt, trying to rein in her impatience enough to keep from ripping off the buttons. He had a meeting later, she reminded herself. He had to wear this shirt. But if it didn't come open soon, he was going to have to go to his meeting wearing only a jacket and tie!

Fortunately for his professional reputation, she was able to remove the garment without damaging it. She threw it aside, not caring if it had a few wrinkles later. "Oh, my," she crooned, spreading her hands over his exceptionally fine chest. "Have I mentioned that you are the most beautiful man in the world?"

He lifted his head from a thorough exploration of the scoop of her T-shirt. "Are you trying to embarrass me again?"

Sliding her fingers into his luxuriously thick hair, she asked, "Does it embarrass you to hear that you're beautiful?"

"Real men aren't supposed to be beautiful."

"I know. It really ticks me off that you're prettier than I am. But I'm getting over it."

Trevor chuckled, shaking his head in exasperation. "Would you be quiet? I'm supposed to be giving the compliments. I'm trying to seduce you here."

She grinned and cupped his face between her hands. "Uh, Trev? Maybe you haven't realized this, but I'm pretty well seduced already."

He unsnapped the waistband of her skirt and began to ease it down her hips, revealing skimpy bikini panties. "I should have known," he said conversationally, "that you wouldn't even take this seriously."

Lifting her head, she kissed him. "Trust me, Trev. I am taking this *very* seriously."

"I'm glad to hear that," he murmured, tugging at her shirt.

Even Jamie found it hard to be amused when Trevor kicked off the rest of his clothes, tossed aside her lacy undergarments and then, finally, brought them flesh-to-flesh. The sound that escaped her more closely resembled a gasp than a laugh.

Trevor's rough groan vibrated through her. "I have to warn you," he muttered, "it's been a long time. I can't guarantee fireworks."

"Don't you know," she asked as she snuggled more closely against him, "that every time you kiss me, I see fireworks?"

He smoothed his hand down her bare side. "How is it that you always seem to know exactly what I need to hear?"

"I only say what I think."

"I know. That's one of the things I've always liked best about you." His hand closed over her right breast, kneading gently. "One of the things," he repeated, his voice going hoarse.

Sliding one smooth leg against his rougher one, she smiled shakily. "Are you saying you admire both my mind and my body?"

He didn't smile in return. "I admire everything about you, Jamie Flaherty."

Almost unbearably touched by his sincerity, she wrapped herself around him. "Let me show you how much I admire you in return, Trevor McBride."

She hadn't been joking when she'd said she didn't need seduction—but she suspected Trevor needed it very badly. Not because he was hesitant about what they were doing—it was more than obvious that he was willing and ready—but because he needed, just for a little while, not to be the one in control. The one responsible for everyone else's happiness and well-being.

Pushing at his shoulders, she shifted and rolled until he was on his back and she was draped over him. "This time," she murmured, "is for you."

He tried a time or two to take charge again, but she was adamant, holding his arms when he would have reached for her, placing her fingers over his mouth when he would have spoken. "Let me make love to you," she whispered.

And then she did, nibbling and kissing her way from his lips to his earlobes and down his jaw to his chin. She pressed openmouthed kisses on his throat, enjoying the frantic beating of his pulse beneath her lips. And then she moved lower to taste the nipples nested in a dusting of golden hair. His breath caught sharply in his throat when she wriggled even lower.

"Jamie…"

"Did I mention," she asked, stroking him admiringly, "that you are absolutely perfect?"

He was also very strong, as he proved when he suddenly hauled her upward and rolled her beneath him, the move accomplished almost before she knew what he intended. He couldn't play anymore, she realized. He needed—and so did she. His hands were shaking when he donned protection, trembling so badly that he fumbled with the task. The uncharacteristic curse he muttered beneath his breath made her giggle.

"If you're laughing at me," he warned, bringing his mouth back to hers.

"I'm laughing with you," she assured him, gathering him close.

"I'm not laughing," he growled, but she saw a faint smile on his lips just before he kissed her.

Then he took her breath completely away when he buried himself deeply, completely inside her.

He hadn't promised her fireworks, but he gave them to her, anyway.

By the time her heartbeat had slowed to near-normal and her breathing had returned to a more regular rhythm, she knew there would be no going back. Before today, she had been able to avoid the L-word, even to herself, when describing her feelings about Trevor. Now it was no longer possible to resist admitting that she was head over heels in love. She had probably been in love with him since the day he'd kissed her behind the school gym fifteen years ago.

Jamie had always had a strong belief in fate. And she knew now that Trevor was hers.

As for whether she was his—well, that remained to be seen.

TREVOR WAS LYING on his back, staring at the ceiling, his right arm around her, her cheek cradled on his damp shoulder. He hadn't said anything since a choked cry had erupted from him during their love-making. Jamie had no clue what was going through his mind. She lifted her head and propped her cheek on her hand. "You know how annoying it is when someone asks what you're thinking?"

He looked at her. "Yeah?"

"Prepare to be annoyed."

He reached up to smooth her hair. "You want to know what I'm thinking?"

"As long as it's flattering to me."

Chuckling, he threaded his fingers through her hair. "I was thinking that I'm very glad you invited me to lunch today."

"Okay," she said after a moment. "I'll take that as a compliment."

"If it's not enough, I have a list of other compliments for you."

"Hang on to them. I'll want to hear them all later." She bent her right leg at the knee, sliding it onto his. "I have a few for you, too, but I wouldn't want to make you conceited."

"There are some who might say you're too late."

She thought of the flashes of uncertainty she had glimpsed in his eyes. The fleeting hints of self-doubt. Things she hadn't seen in him when he was younger. Something had shaken him badly since then, something that had hurt him, stolen the laughter from him. At first she had thought it was the shock and grief of his wife's death. She had begun to wonder if there was something else. For one thing, he *never* mentioned his wife, not even in passing, and that seemed strange to her.

Of course, now was hardly the appropriate time to ask about her.

What was he feeling now? She had made him laugh and then made him groan in pleasure, but what had aroused the renewed somberness she sensed in him? Not regret, perhaps, but guilt, maybe? Wariness about what the future held for them?

She wanted to see him smile again. She walked her fingers up his rib cage, searching for a ticklish spot. She found one about an inch below his armpit. He jerked sharply and she laughed. "Ticklish, Trev?"

"No."

She flicked the area again with the tips of her fingers. And, again, he flinched.

"Liar," she said.

He caught her wandering hand. "Don't make me retaliate."

"You're much too gentlemanly to do anything like that."

"You think so?"

"Of course. Everyone knows that Trevor McBride is the perfect Southern gentleman. Charming, polite, genteel—Trevor! Stop that!" She dissolved into helpless giggles when he flipped her over and tickled her with both hands.

He was grinning, she noted in satisfaction, even as she squirmed to get away from him. He looked relaxed and happy again. A little tickle-retaliation was a small price to pay to see him that way.

Tickling, of course, led to hugging, which led to kissing and then more. By the time Trevor reluctantly dragged himself from the bed, he had little time to wash up and dress for his meeting.

Wrapped in a short robe, Jamie followed him to the front door. He paused before opening it to don his jacket. She reached up to straighten his collar.

"How do I look?" he asked with a smile.

"Great," she assured him. "Like you've spent the entire afternoon rolling around between the sheets."

"That isn't exactly the image I had in mind," he said dryly.

She laughed and gave his tie a final pat. "It's the image I'll keep in *my* mind."

He kissed her quickly. "So will I." And then he stepped away. "I'll call you."

"Do that." She reached for the doorknob. "Now go, before you're late for your meeting."

"See you, Jamie."

"See you, Trev." She hoped she would be seeing him very soon.

EMILY AND WADE had invited Trevor and his family to join them at Sidney Applegate Park for a picnic Thursday after work. It was a beautiful summer day, still warm and bright when they arrived. Trevor knew the kids didn't mind the heat, and he'd changed into a T-shirt and khaki shorts, so he was comfortable enough. With the strap of the diaper bag over his shoulder and Abbie balanced on his hip, he dragged a wheeled cooler full of canned juices and soft drinks behind him, telling Sam to stay close until they found the others.

Even for a weekday afternoon, the park was crowded. Noisy, too, he noted, identifying at least four different types of music sounding from the boom boxes scattered around the area. Sam was bouncing with eagerness to get on the playground equipment; Trevor would be surprised if the boy could sit still long enough to eat. Abbie was just happy to be outside, watching the activity around them.

"There's Aunt Emily and Uncle Wade!" Sam pointed, his voice squeaking in excitement. "And, Daddy, look—it's *Jamie!*"

Trevor almost stumbled, but recovered quickly. Jamie was definitely there, standing close to Emily. She looked wonderful, her red hair glittering in the afternoon sun, her fascinating face animated with laughter, her slender figure flattered by a snug T-shirt and denim shorts. He had never seen her really dressed up, he realized, but she wore her casual wardrobe with an elegance and flair that most women could only envy. She didn't dress "New York"—he'd never seen her in black or wearing trendy labels, the type of outfits Melanie had favored. He wondered if Jamie had dressed this way in New York, or if she'd adjusted her style to fit into Honoria.

What was he doing standing here analyzing her wardrobe? He didn't care about clothes. It was more likely an attempt to distract himself from memories of the last time they'd been together, alone in her bedroom. To stop him from closing the distance between them and tugging her into his arms, right there in front of whoever might see them.

He watched as Sam dashed to her side, eagerly grabbing her hand. Jamie looked down at the boy with one of her blinding smiles, and Sam beamed back up at her. Trevor swallowed hard, identifying a bit too well with the infatuation on his son's face. He'd been doing very well so far keeping his relationship with Jamie completely separate from his other life. He hadn't intended to change that.

He should have known it wouldn't be possible for long in Honoria.

There was no evidence of self-consciousness in her expression when she greeted him. "Hey, Trev. How's it going?"

Aware that his family was watching them, Trevor nodded pleasantly. "Fine, thank you. And you?"

"Can't complain. Hello, beautiful." She tickled Abbie's chin.

The baby laughed and held out her hands, demanding to be transferred. *Even Abbie*, Trevor thought in resignation, handing over his daughter. Jamie hoisted Abbie high in front of her, making the little girl laugh and kick her sneakered feet in delight.

Looking pleased with herself, Emily rested a hand on her cousin's arm. "I'm glad you could come, Trevor."

He brushed a light kiss against her cheek. "You look lovely, as always."

"And you are charming, as always." She motioned toward Jamie, who was skillfully dividing her attention between Abbie, Sam and Clay, who had gravitated to her side with the others. "Isn't it a nice surprise to see Jamie?"

"Yes, it certainly is."

"She and I ran into each other at the bank this afternoon, and I asked if she would like to join us."

"That was nice of you." He made sure to keep his mixed feelings hidden behind a bland smile.

Wade, who'd been setting plastic containers of

food out on a large concrete picnic table, joined them. "Hey, Trevor."

"Hey, Wade. You haven't gotten into the food yet, have you?"

"No, I've managed to stay out of it so far. Emily threatened to whup me if I even took a bite of anything."

Trevor chuckled and glanced down at his petite cousin. "I have no doubt that she could do it."

"Neither do I. That's the only thing that's kept me out of those containers. But I'm warning y'all, I can't wait much longer. I'm starving."

Seeing that Jamie was still occupied with the children, Trevor turned his attention to the baby girl lying in an elaborate stroller next to the picnic table and looking around with wide eyes. "How's Claire?" he asked, lightly stroking her downy hair.

"Growing like a pretty weed," Wade reported proudly. "Won't be long before she's running around playing with the rest of the kids."

"I can't wait to see our newest family member," Emily murmured. "I'm looking forward to going to Atlanta this weekend to visit Tara and Blake and the baby."

"I'm still having trouble picturing Blake as a father."

Emily giggled. "You know Blake will be great— even if he isn't exactly...well, average."

"So, are we just going to stand here and gab, or are we going to eat?" Wade asked, eyeing the food containers with growing impatience.

His wife sighed and shook her head. "Honestly,

Wade. Anyone would think you haven't eaten in days."

"It's been hours. I'm hungry," he said plaintively.

"So am I," Trevor agreed.

Clay had joined them just in time to pipe in, "I'm hungry, too."

"Then I suppose we'd better eat," Emily said matter-of-factly.

A few chaotic minutes later, they were all gathered around well-filled plates of food. Wade, Emily and Clay sat on one side of the table. Sam had scrambled between Trevor and Jamie on the other side. Holding Abbie on his knee, Trevor managed through experience to feed himself and his daughter at the same time. Not that he was as hungry as he'd claimed to be. With Jamie sitting so close to him, it was hard to think of food.

Conversation during the meal was suitably casual, pretty well dominated by the children. He and Jamie put on what he thought was a creditable show of acting like mere acquaintances, though occasionally their gazes met and held for a few moments over Sam's head. He wasn't sure their ruse fooled Wade—not much escaped the sharp-eyed cop—but maybe they'd managed to keep Emily guessing.

He glanced across the table, saw his cousin's smile, and knew he was only fooling himself.

"We're going to the beach," Clay announced loudly, drawing Trevor's attention away from his own thoughts.

"The beach? That sounds great," Jamie said encouragingly. "Where?"

"Alabama. My aunt—Dad's sister—and her husband have a beach house there and we're going to spend a whole week with them."

Jamie looked at Wade with dramatically widened eyes. "The police chief's going to be gone for a whole week? Whatever will we do? Honoria might be hit with a crime wave."

"I've told my deputies to keep an eye on you," Wade drawled without missing a beat, making Emily, Trevor and Clay chuckle and Jamie wrinkle her nose at him.

"I'm through eating, can I go play?" Sam asked.

Trevor glanced at his son's plate, decided he'd eaten enough, and nodded. "Stay close."

"Want to throw my Frisbee with me, Jamie?" Sam offered.

"Jamie hasn't finished eating," Trevor murmured.

But Jamie had already set her plastic fork down. "I've had plenty. I would love to play Frisbee with you, Sammy."

Trying not to look as eager as his younger cousin, Clay stood. "I guess I'll play, too," he said as though he was granting them a favor.

"The more the merrier," Jamie assured him.

"She's wonderful with children, isn't she?" Emily said, watching Jamie frolicking with the boys a few minutes later.

Dragging his gaze away from Jamie, Trevor focused on Abbie, who was playing with a plastic spoon and babbling contentedly to herself on his knee. "Yes, Jamie's very good with children."

"Sam is obviously crazy about her. He completely forgets to be shy when Jamie's around."

"*Shy* is hardly a word in Jamie Flaherty's vocabulary," Wade commented dryly.

"How is he doing with the new nanny?" Emily asked.

Trevor steadied Abbie when she climbed to her feet on his lap, holding on to his head for balance. "Sarah's changed her approach with him, and it's working. He's communicating much better with her."

He didn't add that Jamie had helped there, too.

"I'm glad you and Jamie have been seeing each other," Emily confided, ignoring her husband's meaningful throat clearing. "You make such a nice couple."

"I suppose you've been talking to Mother," Trevor said in resignation.

His cousin giggled. "Are you kidding? Everyone's talking about you and Jamie."

"Emily," Wade murmured.

She looked at him with a shrug. "Well, they are."

Trevor recovered enough voice to ask, "Just what is 'everyone' saying?"

Emily frowned a little, as if she had suddenly become aware that Trevor wasn't pleased. "Uh—not much. Just—well, everyone knows you've been going out on Friday nights—"

So much for those long drives to out-of-town nightspots, Trevor thought grimly.

"...and that you've had lunch at her house several times," Emily added ingenuously.

Trevor winced when Abbie grabbed his hair with both hands and pulled, but his reaction was due more to his cousin's words than to his daughter's actions. He reached up to disentangle her fingers. "Where did you hear *that*?"

"About your lunches? You know Gloria Capps lives across the street from Jamie, don't you?"

Trevor hadn't known his visits had been monitored. He scowled, uncomfortable with the thought that someone had been watching her house while he was there feeling safely alone with her.

The crowded park suddenly looked different to him, making him feel as though everyone was watching him, speculating about him and Jamie. He wondered how many people were watching Jamie romping with Sam and picturing her as a stepmom. That was something he hadn't even considered, he assured himself. He was no more interested in remarrying now than he had been before he'd started seeing Jamie. He doubted that she was interested, herself.

"Now, Trevor, don't start getting all freaked out," Emily chided him. "You know you can't sneeze in this town without everyone knowing about it. They're going to talk about you, whatever you do, so you might as well accept it."

"I don't have to like it," he grumbled.

"No. I hated it that so many people loved spreading unfounded rumors about my brother. But just when I had convinced myself I wanted to move away, I was reminded of all the good things about living here. The low crime rate, the good schools, the way the same people who love to gossip about you will line up to help if you're in trouble."

"And I thought you decided to stay in Honoria only because I moved here," Wade said.

She smiled at him. "That was a definite incentive."

Their attention was distracted when little Claire woke in her stroller with a sudden squawk, and then made it clear that as long as she was awake, she might as well eat. While Emily gave the baby a bottle and Wade began to gather picnic supplies, Trevor busied himself with his increasingly restless daughter.

"Down," Abbie demanded, pointing toward the ground.

"Want to walk?" he asked her.

"Down," she repeated.

He stood, set the child on her feet and held her hands while she tried out her amusingly wobbly legs. Every time he let go of her hands, she fell flat on her diapered bottom. Each time, she laughed, clapped her chubby hands, then held them up for him to do it again.

"I'm not sure she's getting the hang of this walking thing," Jamie commented as she approached them. She sounded slightly winded from her game with the boys, who had turned their attention to trying to pin Wade to the grass.

"I've decided I'm going to have to carry her to kindergarten," Trevor answered wryly, trying not to stare at Jamie's attractively flushed cheeks and bright eyes. The more he looked at her, the more he wanted her. And this was a damn inconvenient time to deal with that.

"She'll walk when she's good and ready, won't you, Abbie?"

"Go," Abbie answered, holding her hands up again.

Somehow Trevor found himself holding Abbie's left hand while Jamie held her right. Supporting the toddler between them, they escorted Sam to the playground equipment, where they took turns entertaining Abbie and supervising Sam's play.

Trevor knew any interested onlookers must think they looked really domestic. Anyone who didn't know them would think they were already a family. Jamie seemed to fit the role very well at the moment.

But then, so had Melanie, a cruel voice inside his head whispered. Most people had thought Melanie was the perfect wife and mother. They hadn't known her at all, of course. And Trevor, perhaps, had been the most deluded about her. He'd thought she was damn near perfect, himself. So perfect that he'd even secretly found her a little dull at times, though he had tried very hard not to acknowledge those uncomfortable feelings.

He'd made himself a promise that he would never be so gullible about a woman again. Nor quite so trusting. He owed it to his children as much as he did to himself.

# 10

THE SHADOWS HAD GROWN long and the sky was beginning to darken by the time the picnic ended. They had finished up, having devoured the cupcakes Jamie had hastily baked after Emily invited her to join them. On the other side of the table, Claire was asleep in Emily's arms, while Clay leaned comfortably against his father. Abbie was beginning to doze against Trevor's chest, and Sam, worn out from running and playing, had crawled into Jamie's lap.

Listening to something Emily was saying, Jamie looped her arms loosely around Sam and rested her cheek against his damp hair. He smelled of little boy, she found herself thinking, an interesting combination of heat and sweetness. It was a nice feeling to sit with this close family, cradling a contentedly drowsy child in her lap.

She glanced at Trevor, whose strong arms so easily supported his little daughter. It had been interesting watching him in this different mode. Not as her date or her lover—the word still evoked sensual memories in the back of her mind. But as a devoted father. He seemed so comfortable in that role. She'd watched him matter-of-factly feed Abbie, entertain her, change her diaper, wipe her hands before and after her cupcake, his movements so confident, his big hands so gentle. She'd watched him roughhouse with Sam, laughing and tickling, tossing the little boy in the air and then catching him so securely.

Loving father. Dutiful son. Caring friend. Passionate lover. Jamie had seen Trevor in all those roles now, but she knew there was a part of himself he kept hidden from her. From everyone, perhaps? Even as she looked at him then, she saw shadows lurking deep within him that she didn't yet understand.

She had so much still to learn about him. They hadn't talked about his marriage or the life he had led in Washington. She still didn't know exactly why he had moved back to Honoria, or what he planned for the future. She didn't know if he had any thoughts of including her in that future. She hadn't forgotten that it had been Emily, not Trevor, who had invited her to join them here.

Glancing her way, he caught her studying him. He gave her a smile that revealed nothing of his thoughts. "I think we've worn the kids out," he announced to all the adults.

Wade groaned. "I thought it was the other way around."

Emily smiled. "As much as I've enjoyed this, it probably is time to call it a day."

"Not yet," Sam protested. "I want to go down the slide again. I'm not tired." But even as he spoke, he yawned and rubbed his eyes.

Jamie chuckled and gave him a hug. "You never get tired, do you, Sammy?"

He grinned sheepishly up at her. "Well...maybe a little."

"We'll come back to the park another time, son," Trevor said. "The slide will still be here."

Sam turned to his father. "Can Jamie come, too?"

"Of course she can."

Even though Trevor had answered without hesitation, Jamie felt a slight frisson of uneasiness go through her. There'd been something in his voice...

"Help me gather everything up, Clay," Wade said, standing and officially bringing the picnic to an end. "Make sure all the trash is in the canisters."

"I'll help," Sam offered, sliding off Jamie's lap.

It didn't take long for all evidence of the meal to be removed, the supplies stowed away and the children hugged, kissed and buckled into their respective seats. Jamie thanked Emily and Wade for including her, waving to them as they drove off. And then she turned to Trevor, who stood beside the unopened driver's door of his car.

"I had a good time," she told him. "I hope you don't mind that Emily invited me."

"Why should I have minded?"

She decided to let him answer that for himself. "Are we still on for tomorrow evening?"

He nodded. "My folks are going to watch the kids again. Then we're all going early Saturday to visit Tara and Blake and the baby."

Which meant, Jamie interpreted, that he probably wouldn't be staying very late at her house. She would just have to make good use of the time they had together. "Why don't I cook dinner for us tomorrow? We can watch a video or play cards or something instead of going out."

It was the "or something" that she was actually offering, of course, and Trevor probably knew it. He nodded. "That sounds nice."

She would have loved to kiss him goodbye, and it wouldn't have mattered to her if half the population of Honoria saw them. But because she knew it mattered to Trevor, she took a step backward. "'Bye, Trev."

He already had one hand on his door handle, prepared to join his children in the car. "Drive carefully."

"I will." Maybe she was just tired, she thought, taking another step away. Maybe that was the reason she was suddenly feeling a little depressed.

"Jamie?"

She looked over her shoulder. "Yes?"

Trevor's faint smile was crooked. "I enjoyed being with you today. I'm glad you came."

Her heart suddenly lighter, she returned the smile with a bright one of her own. "So am I."

"See you tomorrow." He slid into his car and closed the door, though he didn't drive away until Jamie was safely in her own vehicle.

*I enjoyed being with you today. I'm glad you came.*

The encouraging words kept her company as she drove home.

WHEN JAMIE'S DOORBELL rang Friday evening, she rushed to answer it, rather surprised that Trevor was early. He was usually predictably punctual. It pleased her that he'd been impatient to see her.

But Trevor wasn't the recipient of her bright smile

when she threw open the door. "Hello, Clark. Have I forgotten we were supposed to meet this evening?"

"No. I stopped on my way home from the office, and I promise I'll only bother you for a minute. I need your signature on a form. It's one we overlooked earlier. My mistake, I'm afraid."

"Come in," Jamie offered, holding the door wider. "How have you been?"

"Hanging in," he said with a shrug, stepping past her into the living room.

She closed the door. "And your boys?"

"They're doing as well as can be expected, considering that our family is in the middle of a breakup."

She didn't know what to say in response to his bitter tone. To her relief, Clark made it unnecessary for her to say anything. He reached into the pocket of his jacket and pulled out a neatly folded sheet of paper. "I'm sure you have plans for the evening, and I promised not to hold you up for long. You need to sign at the bottom of the page, on the line I marked with a red X."

"Have a seat. Would you like some coffee while I read this?"

He looked tempted. "I don't..."

"The coffee's already made," she assured him.

"In that case, yeah, I'd like a cup."

She smiled. "I'll be right back."

Settling on the couch, he loosened his tie. "Take your time."

Jamie glanced at her watch on the way to the kitchen. She still had half an hour or so before Trevor was due to arrive. It was a good thing she'd been ahead of schedule this evening for a change.

"I forgot to ask if you take anything in your coffee," she said a few minutes later, carrying a filled mug back into the living room.

"No, I take it black." He smiled as he accepted the cup from her. "Thanks."

She sank onto the couch beside him and picked up the form he'd laid on the coffee table. Clark sipped his coffee while she looked it over, asked a couple of questions, and then signed it with the pen he handed to her. She returned the pen and folded the form along its original lines.

"Good coffee," Clark said, setting the mug on a coaster.

She smiled. "You look a bit more relaxed now."

"Yeah. It's been a stressful day. First chance I've had since breakfast to sit down and unwind a little."

"The high-powered life of a small-town accountant," Jamie murmured.

He made a face at her. "I know mockery when I hear it," he said, but showed no sign of offense.

"Not mockery," she assured him. "I was just teasing."

"Jamie Flaherty's specialty."

She shrugged. "I just can't resist sometimes."

He turned on the couch, resting one arm on the back. His jacket parted, revealing his pudgy middle, ruining the studly pose he seemed to be attempting. "You always make me smile, I'll give you that. I enjoy spending time with you, Jamie."

A warning bell rang in her mind. Apparently, she

was slipping. She usually sensed when someone was going to make a move on her. She'd assumed Clark saw her as no more than a friend and client. Sure, they'd flirted a little, but she'd kept it light and impersonal. At least, she thought she had.

"I enjoy being with you, too, Clark," she said briskly. "It's nice when you can be friends and professional associates."

"Maybe we could have dinner one night next week? I mean, since we enjoy spending time together and we're already friends..."

Clark must have been one of the few people not plugged into the Honoria grapevine. Either that, or he was ignoring reports that she had been seeing Trevor. "Thank you for asking, Clark, but I—"

The doorbell cut into her tactful reply. Trevor was early, after all. What interesting timing.

"That will be my dinner guest," she said, standing. "And, Clark—it's Trevor McBride."

He grimaced, his arm falling to his side. "Oh, boy."

"Be nice," she said, pointing a warning finger at him. "This is not a courtroom and you aren't adversaries here."

Clark stood and slipped the form back into his jacket pocket. "I'll be going. There's no way I can make small talk with that bloodsucker."

Resisting an impulse to roll her eyes, Jamie opened the door. "Hi, Trev."

"Whose car is that—oh." Trevor's face hardened when he spotted Clark over her shoulder.

Apparently keeping Jamie's instructions in mind, Clark nodded stiffly. "Trevor."

Trevor hadn't been given orders to "be nice."

"What are you doing here?"

"Clark is here on business," Jamie interceded quickly. "He was just leaving."

Trevor stepped into the room, clearing the doorway. "Don't let me detain you."

Clark turned pointedly to Jamie. "Thanks for the coffee."

She nodded. "Give me a call if there's anything else I need to sign. I'd be happy to stop by your office and save you a trip."

It was a gentle hint, but she hoped it got through.

From the way Clark's mouth twisted, she assumed it had. "Good night, Jamie."

He exchanged a hard look with Trevor on his way out, but they refrained from further comments, to Jamie's relief.

She turned to Trevor after Clark left. "Well. That was pleasant."

"Did you know he was coming?"

"No. He stopped on his way home. He had a form for me to sign."

"Was that his excuse?"

"He had a form for me to sign," she repeated firmly.

"I hope you read it very carefully."

His suspicious tone might have been amusing if he hadn't looked so grim. "I read the form," she assured him. "Now, would you like dinner, or would you rather stand here and bash my accountant?"

Though he looked tempted by the latter, he motioned toward the kitchen. "Let's eat."

Jamie wasn't sure he'd ever remember what he'd eaten. He spent most of the meal studying her across the table, answering her comments in monosyllables.

"I'm beginning to wonder if I should wave a hand in front of your face to see if anyone's there," she commented after yet another conversational gambit died for lack of input on his part.

"I'm listening to you," he defended himself.

"I know you're listening, but you aren't responding. Is there something on your mind this evening? Something bothering you?"

He looked down at his plate. "No."

"Are you annoyed with me about something?"

"Of course not."

"PMS?"

He gave her a look. "Cute."

"Well, come on, Trev, you've hardly said a dozen words since you got here."

"I'm sorry if I've been rude."

"You haven't been rude. Just...distant."

"Then I'm sorry I've been distant."

"Are you sure there isn't something you want to talk about?"

He glanced up at her. "I'd like to tell you to be careful around Clark Foster, but something tells me you wouldn't take it too well."

"You're right," she agreed equably. "I would probably point out to you—again—that Clark is my friend and my accountant."

"Even if I warned you again that he isn't exactly a choirboy? That it was because of his fooling around that his wife is divorcing him?"

"I would tell you again that his divorce is none of my business. And that I am perfectly capable of taking care of myself with men."

"Then I won't say any of the above," Trevor conceded. "I don't want to quarrel with you this evening."

"Neither do I." She smiled at him. "So I'm really glad you've decided not to mention Clark. Would you like dessert? I made peach cobbler."

"Peach cobbler?" His frown lightened.

"It's still warm. And I have ice cream."

That almost made him smile. "I suppose I could eat a little more."

She chuckled and got up from the table. "I'll dish it up. Help yourself to coffee."

"Want me to pour you a cup?"

"Yes, please."

The peach cobbler and ice cream seemed to put him in a better mood. Jamie made a mental note that sweets were a way to perk him up. By the time he had polished off a generous helping, he was almost cheerful.

"So what would you like to do now?" she asked when the cobbler had been devoured and the dishes cleared away. "Watch TV? Play Scrabble? Wash your car?"

"I think we can come up with something more interesting than any of those options—particularly the latter."

The way he was suddenly looking at her made her smile and move closer to him. "We could always alphabetize my pantry."

He slipped his arms around her waist. "Try again."

Looping her arms around his neck, she pretended to give it some thought. "Organize my sock drawer?"

"Do you keep your socks in your bedroom?"

"Of course."

His mouth crooked into a smile. "Why don't we go in there and discuss it?"

"Why don't we?" she murmured, rubbing her lips lightly against his.

They never got around to organizing the sock drawer, of course. And Jamie soon discovered that sweets weren't the only way to put Trevor in a good mood.

TREVOR LEFT much sooner than either of them would have liked. He had no choice, of course, since he had to pick up the children. They were leaving early the next morning to go visit Tara in Atlanta. What bothered her, though, was that it hadn't even seemed to occur to him to invite Jamie along. She told herself not to be offended. Trevor was obviously concentrating on establishing a relationship with her before introducing her into his family. That made sense, she supposed—but she had really enjoyed the family picnic, and she would love to be included again.

But she could wait, she told herself, until he was ready. Or at least until her limited patience ran out completely.

He kissed her lingeringly at the door. "I'll call you."

"Drive carefully tomorrow."

"I will."

"And give my best to your sister and her husband and their new baby."

For some reason, he frowned again—just a little—but he nodded. "I'll do that."

"Good night," she said, trying to keep the wistfulness out of her voice.

He kissed her again. "Good night, Jamie."

As Jamie locked the door and prepared to get ready for bed, she realized that she was missing Trevor already, wondering when she would see him again. It was a little scary how hard she had fallen for him. How much she suddenly had at stake.

She had come back to Honoria when she'd realized that something was missing from her life. She'd thought facing her past, and reexamining her roots would help her identify what she needed to fulfill her. It wasn't money—she could have gone on making a decent income in New York. More than she made here, actually. It wasn't fame, though there had been a time when she'd fantasized about that, too—before she'd realized that she wasn't destined for superstardom. She was too private and independent for that sort of fishbowl life, anyway.

One of the first things she had done when she came back was to revisit the old house on the edge of town where she had grown up. Someone had taken pains to repair the signs of neglect her parents had left behind when they'd moved away. The little house bore new siding, shutters and shingles, and the carport had been enclosed to make a garage. It was obvious that whoever lived there now took pride in the place. But Jamie had been unable to appreciate the improvements. She had looked at the house and had remembered the unhappiness she'd known there. She'd spent a long time parked on the side of the road, staring at the darkened windows, and putting those memories to rest.

Since then, she had found fulfillment here in several ways. Her teaching job—the chance to be a positive influence in so many students' lives, the opportunity to encourage their creativity and talent. Her participation in the fledgling community theater—a chance to be actively involved in the community, to encourage the arts in Honoria. The new friends she had made and the old ones she had reconnected with.

And she had fallen in love.

She had watched Emily and Wade having their picnic with their children yesterday, and she'd found herself envying them. Wondering if she would ever have what they'd found—commitment, security, children.

She wondered if there was even the slightest chance that she would have those things with Trevor.

He'd had it all before. She realized that, and she was honest enough to admit to herself that it bothered her sometimes. Mostly because she knew so little about his marriage. Had he loved his late wife so much that he would never recover, never love anyone else that much again?

He wanted her—she could hardly doubt that now—but could he ever love her?

HIS SISTER SEEMED happier than Trevor had ever seen her. She looked both beautiful and relaxed, he decided. Less driven than she had been only a couple of years ago. Losing her job with a stuffy old legal firm, meeting her unpredictable P.I. husband, starting her own two-person law firm, having her first child—all the changes had combined to make her look happy, contented and fulfilled.

Trevor was happy for her.

Tara's home was filled with the cheerful noise of family—adults laughing, children babbling, babies fussing. In addition to Trevor, his children and his parents, Emily and her family were there. Everyone wanted to celebrate the newest addition to the McBride family—even if this one's last name was Fox.

When the boys grew restless, Emily and Wade volunteered to take them out for ice cream. They took Abbie, too, leaving Trevor and his parents to visit with Tara and Blake.

Bobbie fretted a bit that little Alison had been exposed to so many people that day, but Tara pointed out that the baby might as well get used to being surrounded by family. As fast at the McBride clan was growing, there were many noisy gatherings ahead.

"I only wish Trent could be here," she added. "Did everyone see the beautiful roses he sent me? And the ridiculously big teddy bear he included for the baby?"

More family talk followed. Then Tara turned to Trevor. "Anything new going on in *your* life lately?"

Glancing suspiciously at his suddenly innocent-looking mother, Trevor replied, "Not much."

Tara gave him her patented big-sister grin. "No new ladies in your life?"

Bobbie, Trevor noted, did everything but look up at the ceiling and whistle to distance herself from this particular topic. "What did Mom tell you?" he asked fatalistically.

"Only that you've been spending a lot of time lately with Jamie Flaherty."

What the hell. "She sends her regards to you and Blake."

"How sweet. Please send mine in return."

"Yes, of course," he answered dryly, preparing to be interrogated.

"I've seen her on TV," Blake commented, looking up from little Alison cradled so securely in his strong arms. "She's certainly attractive."

"Blake's a soap opera buff," Tara explained with a chuckle. "He saw Jamie when she played a visiting vixen on one of his soaps."

"She was good, too," Blake added equably. "She almost broke up Dirk and Velvet on *Private Lives*, and their marriage has survived numerous other near disasters. Then Jamie—her name was Veronica on the show—died in a suspicious skydiving accident. Her body was never recovered, though, so there's always a chance she could come back."

Trevor didn't particularly like hearing that. He didn't take time to analyze the reason—probably because he already knew. "I'm sorry I missed her performances."

"It must have been so exciting living in New York," Tara mused. "I wonder why she moved back to Honoria."

"Her aunt Ellen thinks she was getting exhausted

from the hectic pace there," Bobbie commented, rejoining the conversation. "Jamie's a small-town girl at heart. Once she'd had her fill of the big city, she was ready to return to her roots. Like Trevor."

"You don't think it had anything to do with that scandal that made all the tabloids?" Tara asked.

The silence that followed her casual comment was a heavy one.

Tara cleared her throat. "I take it none of you heard about that?"

"*What* scandal?" Bobbie demanded.

"Way to go, Tara," Blake murmured.

She sent her husband a frown. "I just assumed they'd heard. As busy as the rumor mill is in Honoria, I would have thought they'd have discussed Jamie."

"There was a lot of talk when she first moved back," Bobbie said. "Folks started going on about her parents again, and speculating what her life must have been like in New York. Wondering how she would work out as a teacher and placing bets on how long she would stay. But no one said anything about her being involved in a scandal."

Looking uncomfortable, Tara shifted in her chair. "I guess it was only common knowledge in New York and L.A. I wouldn't have known about it, myself, had Blake not mentioned it back when it happened a year or so ago. And he only paid attention because I had commented that I grew up with Jamie when he pointed her out on the show."

Trevor had waited as long as he could. As much as he detested gossip, as much as he despised tabloid journalism, he was unable to resist asking, "What was this scandal about?"

Tara and Blake exchanged glances, Tara looking remorseful, Blake faintly chiding. "I shouldn't have said anything," she murmured. "I know better than to—"

"Tara," Trevor cut in firmly. "What, exactly, did you hear?"

She sighed. "Apparently, Jamie got in the middle of that nasty divorce between Celia Kelly and Alex Greer last year."

Trevor recognized the names, of course. The two screen-and-stage stars were regulars of the tabloids. Even without following celebrity news, Trevor was aware that they'd had a steamy, very public marriage and an even uglier and more public divorce. "What did Jamie have to do with it?"

"Celia claimed that her husband was having a torrid affair with a starlet he'd met while doing a play in New York. He was photographed several times with Jamie, so the gossip columnists named her as one of the suspects. Several concluded that she was one of several girlfriends Alex had on the side. The truth is, of course, that no one really knows what happened, because Alex and Jamie both declined comment."

"Jamie could probably have parlayed the publicity into a career boost," Blake pointed out. "But she apparently chose not to."

"It had to be a difficult time for Jamie," Bobbie said. "No wonder she was ready to get away from all that and come back to Honoria."

"No gossip or scandals in Honoria," Caleb muttered sarcastically.

Trevor couldn't help remembering the previous evening, when he'd found Jamie having a cozy cup of coffee with Clark Foster—another unfaithful husband in the middle of an unpleasant divorce. The mental connection made him scowl, hating himself for his instinctive distrust, resenting the old, painful memories of Melanie that hovered in the back of his mind.

"I think we've discussed this long enough," Caleb concluded firmly. "It's nothing more than a bunch of tabloid gossip, and we know better than to pay any attention to that sort of garbage. Tara, you shouldn't have repeated it, and Trevor, you should pay no mind to it. Jamie seems like a fine young woman and she doesn't deserve to be discussed behind her back this way."

Tara flushed. "Sorry, Daddy. You're absolutely right, of course."

"My fault, I'm afraid," Blake loyally defended his wife. "Rumors and gossip are a part of my business and I probably pay too much attention to them—which doesn't mean I generally believe them, by the way. Just the opposite, in fact."

Tara looked sheepishly at her brother. "I just really thought you knew…"

"Don't worry about it."

Trevor was relieved that Emily and Wade returned with the children a few minutes later. Emily carried Abbie, while Wade followed with Claire. Clay and Sam dashed in after them, their faces sporting evidence of chocolate ice cream. After that, the conversation veered onto a new path.

Trevor only wished it was as easy to change the direction of his thoughts.

## 11

BY TUESDAY AFTERNOON, Jamie still hadn't heard from Trevor. She managed to keep herself busy, doing some necessary chores around the house, making pages of notes about the play her theater group had decided on, scheduling auditions and making arrangements to use the Honoria Community Center for practices and performances. But she often thought about Trevor and wondered why he hadn't called.

She considered calling him, but decided against it. Whatever problems Trevor was having with their relationship, he was going to have to work them out for himself. Whether he was dealing with his feelings for her, or for his late wife, there was nothing she could do to make it any easier for him. She'd just have to be patient, give him space and be there to listen when he was ready to talk.

Feeling restless, she decided she needed to get out of the house for a while. Though hot, it was too nice a day to sit inside alone, waiting for a phone call that might not come. Wearing a pair of denim shortalls over a brightly striped T-shirt, she strapped on her favorite leather sandals, ran a hand through her hair and turned on the answering machine—just in case.

She didn't really have a destination in mind when she headed out, but she ended up at the new ice-cream parlor on Maple Street. Part of the "revitalize downtown" campaign the chamber of commerce had been pushing for the past couple of years, the parlor had been opened in an old stone-front building that had once been home to a pharmacy and soda bar. So far, the new establishment had proven quite popular.

As she entered, Jamie admired the old-fashioned decor—the Tiffany-style lights, the little round tables with bentwood chairs, the old Coca-Cola and Pepsi prints on the walls, the neon-outlined jukebox prominently displayed in a back corner. The old soda bar had been refinished and polished to a high shine, the brass fittings gleaming. It was like stepping back in time to a slower, easier era, and Jamie could almost feel herself relax as she soaked in the atmosphere.

Most of the little tables were occupied, but she spotted an empty one in the back. She'd taken only a few steps toward it when someone said her name. Turning, she smiled when she recognized Joe Cooper, a biology teacher from the high school. "Well, hi," she said, moving toward his table. "How's your summer going?"

He'd risen when she walked over, and shrugged in response to her question. "I'm working at the community center, supervising the summer sports program. It's okay, but I would just as soon be back at school. How about you?"

"I'm ready to get back to work, myself. Although I am helping a group who want to start a community theater program."

"No kidding? Sit down and tell me all about it. Unless you're meeting someone here?"

"No. I'd love to join you."

He held out her chair for her, then took his own again. A ponytailed blond teenager who'd been in both their classes shyly approached to take their orders. Joe ordered coffee, and Jamie requested a strawberry milk shake. When Joe confessed that he'd always had a secret yen to try acting, she immediately started trying to recruit him to audition for the play. So far, not many men had expressed interest in the group, and she needed to round up some likely prospects.

Someone put money in the jukebox and selected several rocking Elvis Presley numbers. Jamie and Joe scooted their chairs closer together so they could hear each other over "Jailhouse Rock."

"You really should try it, Joe," she urged, leaning encouragingly toward him. "It's a lot of fun."

"I'm afraid I'll make a fool of myself."

She reached out to pat his hand, giving him a bracing smile. "As director, I can assure you I would never let that happen."

"Hi, Jamie!"

She recognized the eager young voice immediately. She turned in her seat, spotting Sam a few feet away. "Well, hi, Sammy. How's it going?" she asked, opening her arms.

He launched himself into them for a hug. "I'm getting ice cream. Chocolate," he announced happily.

"Yum. Where's—oh, there you are, Trev. Hi." Jamie gave him the warm smile she reserved just for him.

He didn't smile back at her. He glanced coldly from

her to Joe and then back again. And then he nodded, as if she were someone he didn't know all that well. "Hello, Jamie."

"Where's Abbie?" she asked, eyeing Trevor thoughtfully.

"She's at Grandma's house," Sam volunteered. "Daddy and me are having a guys' night out."

"I'm sure you're both enjoying that. Joe, have you met Trevor McBride and his son, Sam?"

"No, I haven't." Joe smiled politely and held out a hand. "Joe Cooper. Nice to meet you."

It might have been the briefest handshake in history, Jamie thought, surprised by Trevor's behavior. His acknowledgment of Joe's greeting was only marginally civil. "We'll leave you two to enjoy your desserts. Come along, Sam."

Jamie was still frowning after Trevor in bewilderment when Joe spoke again. "Good friend?" he asked casually.

She turned her gaze back to him. "Yes."

"He, uh, didn't look too happy to see us together."

Forcing a smile, she shook her head. "He's probably just had a rough day. So, are you going to audition for the play or not?"

"You really think I can do it?"

"I'm sure you can."

They continued the conversation for a few minutes more, and then Jamie surreptitiously glanced around in search of Trevor and Sam. She didn't see them. Apparently, they had gotten their ice cream to go.

She wondered what Trevor's problem had been. He couldn't really have been annoyed that she'd been having ice cream with Joe, could he? If so, they needed to have a long talk.

WEDNESDAY MORNING started out badly enough for Trevor, but it had turned into a nightmare when his father collapsed in his office. They had been talking as they always did about their cases, and there had been no indication that anything was wrong until Caleb started to rise. And then he grabbed his chest, groaned and folded to the floor, his face as white as his snowy shirt.

Trevor practically leaped over the desk in his desperation to get to his father. "Dad? *Dad!*"

Still conscious, Caleb moaned and tried to speak, but he wasn't able to form the words.

In panic, Trevor and Marie had called for an ambulance and then had sat in silent prayer until it arrived. Trevor wasn't sure he could handle losing his father now. He wasn't ready for this, he thought sickly. Not by a long shot.

JAMIE HEARD the news about Caleb McBride the way one usually heard things in Honoria—through the grapevine. Her friend Susan called her Wednesday evening. "I wasn't sure you would be home," she said. "I thought you might be with Trevor."

Having spent the day painting and fretting about why Trevor hadn't called, Jamie frowned. "No. He and I usually go out on Friday evenings."

"I didn't think you were on a date, obviously," Susan chided. "Not with his father in the hospital."

"In the hospital?" Jamie repeated weakly.

"You didn't—surely you've heard that Caleb collapsed at work this morning? Word is that he had a heart attack."

"No. I hadn't heard." The admission was painful to make. She couldn't imagine why Trevor hadn't called her. Wouldn't he have known she'd want to be there with him? "Is he—is Mr. McBride—" She couldn't get the words out.

"I've heard he's going to be fine," Susan reassured her quickly. "If it was a heart attack, apparently it was a mild one. Everyone's talking about it, and they all seem confident that he's going to pull through."

"What a relief. He's such a good man. His family would be devastated to lose him." Trevor would be devastated, she added silently.

*Why hadn't he called?*

"Thanks for letting me know, Susan," she added when the silence at the other end of the line stretched too long.

"Sure. I just assumed you already—well, anyway, everything's going to be okay, so there's really no reason to worry about it."

Susan, of course, had assumed Jamie would know that her lover's father was in the hospital. It was a reasonable assumption. Jamie found the fact that Trevor hadn't let her know very difficult to understand, herself.

He'd hurt her before, but cutting her out this time was too much. It was time she found out once and for all just what Trevor wanted from her. And then she would have to decide if what he wanted was enough.

TREVOR WAS RELIEVED when the children were finally tucked into bed and sleeping Thursday night. Abbie had resisted bedtime a little more than usual, which had kept Sam awake, but they'd finally dropped off. Trevor retreated to the living room, turning on the evening news at a low volume. He thought about pouring himself a drink, but he resisted. It had been almost a week since he'd had a drink—he'd decided he was getting a bit too accustomed to those bourbons-in-the-dark.

He never glanced at the telephone, but he was very aware of it sitting nearby in what seemed oddly like silent reproach. His answering machine was on, not that he had returned any calls lately. He hadn't even responded to the two messages Jamie had left him since he'd seen her at the ice-cream parlor Tuesday.

He knew he should talk to her. It was both cowardly and rude to continue to avoid her this way, especially since she was probably expecting to see him tomorrow night, as they had for the past five Friday evenings. He simply hadn't been able to decide what to say to her.

He still wanted her so badly he ached. So badly he felt as if his own heart was being squeezed in his chest. He didn't like to admit that it was fear keeping him away from her—but he knew that it was.

When the phone rang, he grimaced. He had no doubt who was calling. He didn't move, but muted the TV so he could hear her message.

Apparently, Jamie had run out of patience. "Pick up the phone, Trev, or I'm coming over there right now to see if you're dead in the bathtub."

She would, too. After only a momentary hesitation, he sighed and lifted the receiver, telling himself to stop being a damn coward. "I'm not dead."

"Well, that's a relief." She sounded satisfied that she'd finally reached him.

"I, uh, just got the kids in bed. Abbie was wound up this evening."

"Are the children all right?"

"Yes, they're fine."

"I heard from the usual sources that your father has been ill. In fact, some people seem to think he had a heart attack yesterday morning. I was shocked to hear it, of course—although the person who told me assumed I had already heard." Her voice was as brittle as glass, and he knew she was hurt that he hadn't been the one to tell her.

"It wasn't a heart attack," he clarified quickly. "He had some chest pains and we took him to the hospital, but he was told it was just an 'episode,' whatever that means. He's being put on a restricted diet and an exercise program, and he's going to be closely monitored for the next few months, but he seems to be feeling pretty well today."

"And that happened yesterday morning?"

"Yes. We were at the office." Trevor still hadn't fully recovered from the terror.

"And during all the hours that have passed since, you never had a chance to call and let me know what had happened?"

There had been times he could have called her, of course. Times he'd wanted to call her. Times when he had needed to hear her voice, to feel the reassuring touch of her hand. But he'd resisted, for reasons he couldn't explain to her now, because he didn't quite understand, himself. It had something to do with his concern about becoming too dependent on her. Needing her too much—and then not being able to hold on to her. Or discovering that, like Melanie, she wasn't what she had seemed to be.

He had vowed that he wouldn't get into that situation again. With anyone.

"I can think of only a couple of reasons why you didn't call," she continued when he remained silent. "Either I never crossed your mind, or you thought your family crisis was none of my business. Either way, it doesn't say much for our relationship, does it? Or did it even occur to you that we *have* a relationship?"

He cleared his throat, scowling at the memory of seeing her sitting at that ice-cream-shop table, focusing her warm smile and bright eyes on a handsome, dark-haired man. "You're the one who had a date with someone else just two days ago."

"A date?" Her voice rose in what sounded like disbelief. "I didn't have a date. Surely you aren't talking about the ice cream I had with Joe Cooper, a coworker I happened to run into by accident. The only thing he and I talked about was the community theater, which I would have been happy to tell you about if you'd given me a chance. And as far as commitments go, I made one to you the first time I went to bed with you. Despite what you seem to believe, I don't take that sort of thing lightly."

The hurt he heard in her voice made him react defensively, causing all his emotional baggage to surface. Without pausing to think, he blurted, "Oh, really? So how *did* you end up in the tabloids last year? Something to do with another woman's husband, I believe?"

He heard her breath catch, and he immediately regretted his words. They'd been vicious and unfair—and to make it worse, they had been directed as much at his late wife as they had at Jamie. "Damn it, Jamie, I—"

Her voice was very composed when she interrupted, and he could only imagine how much stage experience it must have taken for her to keep it that way. "Funny," she said. "I would have thought you, of all people, would have known how foolish it is to listen to gossip."

"Let's just say I learned last year that the gossip is sometimes true," he answered bitterly. "My unfaithful wife taught me that painful lesson very well. And I made a promise to myself that I wouldn't be made to look the fool twice."

Jamie digested his revelation in silence for a moment before speaking again. "Whatever problems you had with your wife," she said quietly, "it isn't fair of you to take them out on me."

"You're right." His voice was gruff. "It's just that—well, there was talk of what happened in New York between you and that actor. And then, when I saw you with Clark, and with that guy, Joe..."

"I've been told that I act too friendly sometimes, that my actions could be misinterpreted. That's what happened in New York, by the way. I tried to help a friend through a difficult time and it backfired on me. Maybe the reason I came on so strong with you is that I've always been so damn attracted to you. You seem to have misinterpreted that, too—though you certainly didn't mind taking advantage of it. Maybe you did have a few misconceptions about actors and the wild lives they lead," she mused. "Or maybe you just wanted a woman—any woman—and I was convenient. A little too convenient, it seems."

Trevor imagined that if someone were to measure him with a ruler, he would have shrunk several inches during her quiet speech. She'd made him feel very small—primarily because so many of the things she had said had hit much too close to home. "You don't understand—"

"No. I don't understand, because you haven't talked to me. You've never told me how you feel about me. You've never let me know what, if anything, you wanted from me —besides sex, of course."

He winced.

"I'm sorry," she said again and her voice was almost sad. He wasn't used to hearing Jamie sound that way. "This isn't going to work. I've been deluding myself. Funny, I thought I'd outgrown that since the last time."

*The last time?* "I don't know what you mean."

"When we were teenagers, I convinced myself that we could be together. I thought if I could make you want me, I could make you love me. You decided I was wrong for you then, and you left, without ever looking back at me. This time, I pretended things were different. We were finally in the right place at the right time, or so I wanted to believe. But once again, I was the only one in love. You've had your fun—your kisses behind the gym, in a manner of speaking—and now you're moving on. And once again, I'm going to wish you well and let you go."

*Love.* The word echoed through his mind, nearly drowning out all other thought. He didn't know how to respond.

"This is mostly my fault, of course. The signs were all there, and I chose to ignore them. You never gave me any reason to expect a future with you. You've never made me a part of your life. And I've had the feeling that you've deliberately kept me away from your children."

He frowned then. "I have a responsibility to protect my children."

"You felt you needed to protect them from *me?*"

Again, he detected hurt in her voice, and he imagined himself shrinking another few inches. "I just didn't want them to get too attached to you, in case things didn't work out between us. They've lost their mother—I don't want them to go through anything like that again."

"And you were pretty sure that things wouldn't work out between us, weren't you? You've never expected, maybe never even wanted, anything different. It turns out you never even trusted me. I don't blame you if you can't love me, but I deserved better than to be used as a warm body to ease your loneliness."

She took his silence as a response. "We managed to avoid each other for the first few months after I moved back. I'm sure we can do it again, for the most part. People will talk, of course, and speculate about what happened between us, but something new will come along to entertain them soon."

She was breaking up with him. Writing him off. Putting an end to whatever it was they had found together. And even though he knew it was his own fault, he suddenly panicked. "Jamie, wait—"

"Goodbye, Trevor," she said gently. "It was, well, it was definitely interesting."

She'd called him Trevor. Not the more casual and intimate Trev. He was still trying to come up with the right words when she hung up, leaving nothing but a dial tone in his ear and an empty ache in his heart.

She had replaced her receiver gently. Trevor slammed his home so hard the instrument jangled in protest. And then he grimaced, hoping his tantrum hadn't woken the kids.

He sat for a long time in silence, one hand still resting on the telephone, his eyes fixed on nothing, his thoughts dark and unfocused. He finally stood, grinding a curse out between his teeth. He needed a drink to smooth the edges of the jagged guilt inside him. To ease the regret. To soothe the ache of unfulfilled needs. Maybe to calm the fear.

He picked up the bottle, and reached for a glass. Then he just stood there, unable to move, her words haunting him.

*Once again, I was the only one in love.*

His hand clenched so tightly around the glass that he was surprised it didn't shatter. Moving very deliberately, he set the unopened bottle on a high shelf and put the glass back in the cabinet. And then he turned off the light and sank into his usual chair, his hands fisted on his knees.

He wouldn't numb the pain tonight, he told himself. He deserved to feel it all.

"SHE'S A DELIGHTFUL young woman. Very quiet and refined, exactly what I think you would like. And she loves children. Why don't you give my great-niece a call?" Martha Godwin urged. "I'm sure you'll like her."

Trevor made no effort to be tactful. "I'm really not interested."

Ignoring the people milling around them in the bank lobby where they'd met by accident, Martha shook a finger at him. "You should listen to me, Trevor. You need a wife and those children need a mother. As interesting as Jamie Flaherty is, I'm sure you realize she's hardly—"

Trevor didn't want to hear the end of that sentence. "I have to go. Goodbye, Mrs. Godwin."

"Now, Trevor, I haven't finished talking to you."

Yes, she had. Trevor had no intention of waiting around for more. Ever since word had gotten out that he and Jamie weren't seeing each other anymore, he'd been besieged by elderly women trying to fix him up. Apparently, they had taken his interest in Jamie as a sign that he was ready to date again.

It was hard enough dealing with his own problems without having to put himself at the mercy of the local matchmakers. And he didn't want to meet another woman. Jamie was the only woman he wanted—so badly he wasn't sure he would survive another night without her. And yet he still hadn't found the courage to go after her. To risk hearing her say that she had finally gotten him out of her system, once and for all.

It was a relief to have even the fifteen minutes of solitude he got during the drive across town. It had been two weeks since he and Jamie had split up, and he had reacted to the breakup the same way he'd handled Melanie's death. He'd withdrawn, hiding behind work and his children, trying to keep himself too busy to think. Except in the middle of the night, of course, when there had been nothing left to do except sit in his living room and brood.

He missed her. He missed her quirky observations on life, her near-blinding smiles, her contagious sense of humor. Her generous affection—too generous, he had feared. But when it had been focused solely on him, it had been great. She'd been able to make him laugh, to make him forget. To make him feel alive again. And he missed her.

Even if he could ever convince her to give him another chance—and that was a huge 'if,' considering the things he'd said to her—did he really have the courage to try again? For the children's sake—for his own—should he take the risk again?

He was almost overwhelmed by the urge to say yes. He was fully, angrily aware that it was pure fear that held him back.

JAMIE WAS IMPATIENT for school to start again. As busy as she had kept herself during the two weeks that had passed since Trevor McBride had broken her heart again, it still wasn't enough. She needed to fill more hours. It was the first week of August and teachers were to report back to school in less than three weeks, she reminded herself. As far as she was concerned, the time couldn't pass quickly enough.

She'd been fortunate that she hadn't run into Trevor yet. It was inevitable, of course—Honoria wasn't that big. And she supposed it really didn't matter how much time passed before it happened. For the rest of her life, it was going to hurt to see Trevor McBride and know they would never be together.

They ran into each other, almost literally, at the post office. It was raining, and Jamie had forgotten her umbrella. She jumped out of her car and made a dash for the door, skidding to a stop in a puddle of water just before she crashed into the back of someone.

That someone was Trevor.

Glancing down at her, he immediately shifted his large black umbrella so that it sheltered them both, although Jamie was already wet. For one of the few times in her life, she couldn't think of anything to say. They entered the building in silence. Only when they were inside, out of the rain, did Trevor speak. "It's really coming down, isn't it?"

Oh, God, she thought. They were going to have a polite discussion about the weather. She wasn't sure she could handle that. "Is it? I haven't noticed."

The faintly reproachful look he gave her almost broke her heart again. It was so typical of Trevor. "How have you been?" he asked.

"I've been better," she answered candidly, "but I've been worse, too, so I won't complain."

"Jamie—" He looked suddenly resolute, as if he had just then made up his mind about something. "Let's get out of here. We can have a cup of coffee or something."

He didn't trust her, she reminded herself. He hadn't trusted her even when he had made love with her. And nothing had ever hurt her more. Not the first time he'd rejected her, when he'd said he was leaving for college and wanted nothing to tie him down in Honoria. Not even the day she had heard that he was engaged, or when she'd read his wedding announcement in the local newspaper that she'd always had mailed to her in New York. She could have lived with the fact that he didn't love her, but to know he didn't trust her, that he'd only been using her— that was simply too painful to accept. "No."

His eyes narrowed in that stubborn look of his. "We need to talk."

"We talked," she reminded him. "And, frankly, I didn't enjoy it much."

"Damn it—"

"Goodbye, Trevor. I would ask you to give my love to the children, but I know how important it is for you to protect them from my influence."

Okay, so it was a cheap shot. She figured she deserved a couple. Because she was afraid she would give in to her craven heart and change her mind, she nodded curtly and turned on one heel. He didn't try to stop her when she walked away—and that only hurt her all over again.

# 12

JAMIE WAS EXPECTING a call Friday afternoon. Susan had delivered a healthy baby boy Wednesday night and had expected to be released from the hospital Friday morning. She'd promised to call and report on their progress. When the phone rang, Jamie snatched it up, picturing Susan at home with her son. The image was bittersweet. As happy as she was for her friend, Jamie couldn't help being aware of how slim the chances were that she would ever hold her own child.

She was startled to hear Trevor's voice on the other end of the line. "Jamie. It's Trevor."

Her first instinct was to tell him again that she didn't want to talk to him. She simply couldn't get involved with him again without trust. But something she heard in his voice made her hesitate. "Is something wrong?"

"It's my brother, Trent."

The depth of anguish in his tone struck at her heart. "Oh, God. What's happened?"

"He's been in a plane crash. There's a chance he—"

"I'm so sorry," she said. "What can I do?"

He had recovered his voice, though it was still gruff. "My parents and I are flying to him immediately."

"Of course. Who will watch Sam and Abbie?"

"That's why I called. Can you take care of them for me?"

She was so startled by the question that it took her a moment to answer. "You want them to stay with *me*?"

"Yes. It would be ideal if you could stay here with them, but I'll bring them to you, if that's better for you. I know I'm asking a lot..."

"What about Emily? Or your nanny?"

"Emily's still in Alabama with Wade's family. Sarah left yesterday for a week-long vacation in Florida. Even if Sarah had been in town, I would have called you first. Sam's going to be upset enough that I'm leaving. Having you with him will make it easier for him. But if you'd rather not, there are other people I can call."

"It isn't that I mind. But I've had so little experience with children. I'm afraid I'll do something wrong."

"If I didn't think you could handle it, I wouldn't have asked."

Jamie had to believe him. No matter what their personal history, he would never leave his children with someone he didn't trust to take care of them. "When are you leaving?"

"As soon as we can."

"I'm on my way." There were tears in her eyes when she hung up the phone. She blinked them away and dashed toward the bedroom to throw some clothes in a suitcase. Maybe she was only a convenience for him again, but she could no more have turned him down than she could have flown. He needed her, and so did his children.

Trevor met her at his door less than half an hour later. The expression on his face made her eyes fill again. "Oh, Trev. I'm so sorry," she said, putting her arms around him.

He gathered her close for a fierce hug, and for several long moments they just stood there, holding each other, Jamie offering comfort, Trevor accepting it. He finally drew away. "Abbie's taking a nap," he said roughly. "Sam's in his room. He's upset that I'm leaving, though I think he understands that I have to go. I wrote down everything I could think of that you need to know. I'll call as often as I can."

"We'll be fine," she assured him. "Go to Trent."

He started to speak, then choked. Jamie rested a hand against his cheek. "Your brother's going to make it. I feel it."

"Jamie Flaherty's brand of optimism," he murmured, putting his hand over hers. "I'll try to hold on to it."

"You do that. Do you want to say goodbye to Sam before you go?"

"I've already told him goodbye. And I just looked in on Abbie. I'd better go. My parents are anxious to get to the airport."

"I'll take good care of your children."

"I know you will." He brushed a kiss against her cheek. "When I get back, we're going to have that talk. And this time you're going to listen."

Her heart was in her throat when she watched him pick up the suitcase he'd had waiting by the door and let himself out. She couldn't help being aware that he had turned to her in his time of need. He had trusted her with his children. She would have to give careful thought to what that meant.

She had never even been in his home before, she suddenly realized, turning to look at the room around her. It didn't take her long to find Sam's room. The door was open and Sam was on the bed, holding a stuffed monkey and looking at a picture book. He looked up without smiling. "Is my daddy gone?"

"Yes. He's gone to take care of your uncle Trent." She sat lightly on the edge of the bed, facing him. "He'll be back as soon as he can."

The boy's lip quivered. "My mommy didn't come back."

His barely audible murmur broke her heart. "Your daddy *will* come back, Sam. I'm sure of it."

He seemed to take reassurance from her promise.

"In the meantime," she added bracingly, "you and I are going to take care of Abbie. D'you think we can handle that?"

Straightening his narrow little shoulders, he nodded. "I'll help you," he assured her. "I know what to do."

"I'm glad to hear that," she said. "Because I'm new at this."

A bit tentatively, Sam set the book aside and moved closer to Jamie. She reached out to him, and he burrowed himself into her arms. Holding him close, she rested her cheek on his soft blond hair and felt herself fall helplessly in love all over again.

TREVOR'S HOUSE was quiet when he entered it five days later. He was home several hours before he'd planned to be, since he'd managed to catch an earlier flight than he'd expected. He had looked forward to being greeted by Jamie and the children and was disappointed that they weren't here.

Running a weary hand through his hair, he wandered into the kitchen. Funny how he could almost feel Jamie's presence in his home, even though she wasn't here at the moment. During the hellish days that had just passed, he had derived comfort from imagining her here. And he had decided then that he would do everything in his power to put things right between him. He wanted her, and he needed her. Come hell or high water, he was going to get her back.

He was ready to take the risk of loving her.

There was a note on the refrigerator, he observed immediately. Only one word was written on it, in bold letters, in red crayon: Pool.

She had left him a message, he thought with a faint smile. Just in case he came early. Jamie Flaherty's own special brand of optimism. Only lately had he realized how much he had grown to depend on it.

He walked the few blocks to the pool. Though it was hot, he needed the fresh air to clear away the memory of hospital scents from his mind. Tension still tightened his shoulders—it would be a while before that eased completely—but it felt good to be home.

To his relief, there weren't many people at the pool. The young lifeguard, with whom Trevor had had a long, firm talk after Sam's near tragedy, straightened in his elevated chair when he recognized Trevor.

Trevor immediately spotted Jamie in the pool, her hair wet and slicked back from her face. She had one hand on the molded plastic seat in which Abbie floated happily, and she was talking to Sam—who, Trevor was surprised to notice, was standing waist-deep in water beside Jamie. He was even more astonished when, acting on Jamie's instructions, Sam put his face in the water, kicked off and swam three or four feet in exaggerated, splashing strokes. He sank then, but came up laughing, dripping, and wiping water from his face with both hands.

This from the boy who didn't even like to have his hair washed for fear of getting water in his eyes?

It was Sam who spotted Trevor first. His wet face lit up. "Daddy! Did you see me? I swam."

"I saw you. You were great, Sam. When did you learn to do that?"

"Jamie taught me. She used to be a lifeguard."

Jamie had already lifted Abbie out of the floating seat. Holding the dripping baby on her hip, she carefully climbed the steps out of the pool. She approached Trevor with a smile, Sam at her heels. Seeing Trevor, Abbie squealed and held out her hands. "Daddy!"

Paying no heed to his travel-wrinkled shirt and chinos, he gathered his daughter close and eagerly accepted her slobbery kisses. This, he thought as Sam grabbed on to his leg and hugged fervently, was exactly what he had needed. "How's my princess?" he asked, nuzzling Abbie's warm cheek. "Did Jamie teach you to swim, too?"

"No," Sam said, gazing up at him. "But she walked. All by herself. Without holding on to anything."

Trevor lifted an eyebrow in Jamie's direction. "It sounds as if I've left my children with Mary Poppins."

She smiled, though he couldn't quite read the expression in her eyes. "Not exactly. I have experience teaching swimming, and Abbie was definitely ready to walk, anyway."

He was having to make an effort to keep his eyes focused on her face, rather than the expanse of skin revealed by her hot-pink bikini. He was aware that a hug from Jamie was the only thing missing to make his homecoming complete, but the way she stood let him know that was unlikely. Though she hadn't hesitated to come through for him when he'd needed her, he still had a long way to go to win her forgiveness.

He would not accept that she might never grant it to him.

She reached for her cover-up and pulled it over her head, to Trevor's mingled regret and relief. "How was Trent when you left?" she asked.

"The same. He's out of immediate danger, thank God, but he has a long recuperation ahead of him. It's really a miracle that he wasn't killed."

"Didn't I tell you he would be all right?" she asked with a shadow of her usual smile.

"Yes, you did." Aware of curious eyes focused on

them, Trevor asked, "Are you ready to go home, or do you want to stay a while longer?"

"We're ready," Jamie answered. "The kids have been in the sun long enough."

Trevor pushed Abbie's stroller, Jamie carried the floating seat and Sam skipped alongside them, chattering a mile a minute about the fun he'd had with Jamie. Trevor listened with a pang that he found ironically amusing. As far as he could tell, his children hadn't missed him at all. He supposed he shouldn't be surprised. They couldn't be blamed for falling under Jamie's spell. Everyone else did—including him.

AN HOUR LATER, the children had been bathed, Abbie was tucked into bed for a nap and Sam was parked in front of the TV with a bowl of sliced fruit and his favorite hour-long cartoon video. Jamie had showered and dressed in shorts and an I-Love-New-York T-shirt. Trevor liked the shorts. Hated the T-shirt. It reminded him of his fears that neither he nor Honoria would ever be exciting enough to hold her.

He had coffee ready when Jamie came out of the shower. "I really should go," she said. "I'm sure you can handle things here now."

"Just a cup of coffee before you go," he urged. "You can catch me up on everything I missed."

She nodded with visible hesitation. So, before she could change her mind, he handed her a mug and waved her toward the kitchen table.

"I see your clothes have dried," she commented, stiffly taking a seat.

He glanced down ruefully as he sank into his own

chair. "They look as though I've slept in them for a few days, but they're dry."

"I've always liked seeing you rumpled," she murmured, gazing into her coffee.

It was the kind of remark she might have made to him before their breakup. But she'd said it with such an inscrutable expression that he had no idea what to make of it. And then she immediately changed the subject. "Tell me about Trent. We haven't been able to talk much during the past few days. What's going to happen with him now?"

He rubbed a hand over his face. "He'll be in the hospital for several more weeks. Our parents are going to stay with him until he's released, and they'll bring him home to recuperate as soon as he's able to travel."

"Your family has had to endure so much during the past year."

He knew she was indirectly including Melanie's death in the statement. "We've had our blessings, too," he said, thinking of the babies born, the holidays celebrated, the medical scare his father had survived. "We're all very grateful that we didn't lose Trent."

"What about his air force career?"

"It's over," Trevor said flatly. "All he's ever wanted to do was fly, and now, because of his own recklessness, he'll never be able to do it again."

"His own recklessness?" she repeated with a frown. "The accident was his fault?"

"He was hotdogging. Showing off. Yeah, it was his fault. And he's paid for it by losing his dream. I just hope he can learn to forgive himself for that eventually. He's so bitter about it now that he's hardly even speaking to anyone."

"He'll have to find a new dream," Jamie said, the prosaic words softened by the sympathy in her eyes.

Trevor thought bleakly of lost aspirations, and of the emptiness they left in their wake. "That's easier said than done."

"Trust me. No one knows that better than I do."

"You're referring to acting?"

Her expression distant again, she said, "I've learned to let go of several dreams." Abruptly, she pushed her coffee mug away and stood. "I really should go. I have things to do at home."

He wouldn't—he couldn't—let her go. Not yet. Not without trying to entice her to stay.

She moved so quickly that he barely caught her. Trapping her with his hand on her arm, he said, "Wait. I want to thank you for what you've done this past week. I don't how we would have gotten along without you."

"You're welcome," she said without looking at him. "I've enjoyed the time with the children."

He drew a deep breath. "I want us to be together again, Jamie. The way we were before."

She stiffened. "Regular Friday-night dates?" she asked after a pause. "The occasional nooner at my place? You leading your life and me leading mine? Sorry, that's not good enough for me anymore."

He shook his head impatiently. "That isn't what I meant. I want a real relationship this time. I won't keep you from my kids again."

"That sounds a lot like another arrangement of convenience to me, one that now includes baby-sitting. As much as I love Sam and Abbie, I'm going to have to pass."

"Damn it, Jamie, that isn't what I mean." He wished she would turn to look at him, but she stood rigidly, offering no encouragement. He played his last card with a sense of desperation. "I love you."

She moved then, but not the way he'd hoped. She jerked away from him, taking another step toward the door.

"Jamie," he repeated, just in case she hadn't heard. "I love you."

She wouldn't look at him. "There can't be love without trust."

"There's no one I trust more than you. I hurt you and damn near ruined my own life before it finally sank in, but it's true."

She turned very slowly, her eyes narrowed. Angry. "You didn't just hurt me, Trevor. You devastated me. What makes you think I can ever trust *you* now?"

It was illuminating being on the other side. He hated it. "I—"

"I won't spend the rest of my life trying to prove to you that I'm not like your wife," she said flatly. "I used to worry that she had been too perfect, that I could never live up to her image. Now I'm afraid I could never escape her shadow. It isn't fair for you to put that burden on me. I don't know what she did to you, since you've never talked to me about it, but I won't—"

"There's a chance that Abbie is not my daughter."

The words seemed to have been ripped from his chest. He had never spoken them aloud before, and it was even more painful than he had imagined. Each syllable seemed to slice his throat as it passed through.

The effect on Jamie was dramatic. Her face went pale, her eyes huge. "Oh, Trevor—"

He forced himself to speak again. "I found out after Melanie died that she'd been having affairs. After reading her journal, I realized that even she didn't know exactly who had fathered Abbie. While she was imitating the perfect Stepford wife for me, she was playing around while I was at work, leaving the household to the maids and nannies. I thought she was occupied with charitable activities. Her 'charities' turned out to be married senators. Abbie was three months old when I read that. I already loved her more than my own life, and I still do. I just don't know if she—"

His voice broke.

"Trevor, I'm so sorry. You must have been—"

"Devastated," he supplied, remembering the word Jamie had used earlier. "I had just lost my wife. And then I found out that I hadn't even really known her. And my baby girl—"

She took a tiny step toward him. "You never had a blood test?"

"No. I'm afraid to," he said simply. That cowardly streak of his again. Until Melanie had died, taking his smug illusions of control with her, he'd always thought himself a reasonably bold and confident man.

Jamie was still looking at him. "Do your parents know?"

"No one here knows. There was plenty of talk in Washington. It turned out a lot of people knew Melanie better than I did, and the word got out very quickly that she'd been with one of her senators the day she died—but I've managed to keep it quiet here. What happened was partly my fault, of course. I was too focused on work, too busy with my own ambitions to pay enough attention to her. We played out a predictable little script, saying and doing the right things without either of us taking them seriously enough. I was perfectly content to go on pretending we had an ideal life, without working hard enough to make sure that it really was. But for her not to tell me about Abbie—it's very hard for me to forgive her that."

"And so you decided that no woman could be trusted? Or was that doubt reserved for me?"

Her words were spoken lightly, but their seriousness was obvious by the pain still visible in her eyes.

"I'm sorry." He wished there were more adequate words to express his regret at what he had done to her. "You were right—it wasn't you I was angry with. It was Melanie—and myself. And it was unfair of me to take that out on you. I let my anger and my fears take over, and I was a total jerk. I finally admitted it while I was sitting at my brother's bedside, thinking of how fragile life is, and how much I had thrown away by turning on you the way I did."

"I've suffered a few betrayals, but no one has ever

hurt me the way you did when you all but called me a slut," she said quietly.

He frowned, instinctively rejecting the word. "I didn't—"

"Semantics, Trevor."

He wished she would call him Trev. Or smile for him. He was painfully aware that he had taken the laughter out of her.

"What is it going to take," he asked softly, "for me to earn your trust again? Because whatever it is, I'll do it."

Her reply was unencouraging. "I don't know if you can."

The kitchen door swung open and Sam walked in, blissfully unaware of the tension between the adults. "Abbie's awake. She's calling you, Daddy."

"I'll go get her." He paused and looked at Jamie. "Don't leave before I get back. Please," he added, aware of how arrogant that might have sounded.

"Jamie's staying for dinner," Sam insisted quickly. "She's making spaghetti. Remember, Jamie? You said."

"Well, that was before I knew your daddy would be back so early," Jamie reminded him.

Sam shook his head, his lip jutting out stubbornly. "You said you'd make spaghetti. Daddy likes spaghetti, too."

"I *love* spaghetti," Trevor agreed shamelessly.

The look Jamie gave him should have made him gulp. But then she nodded and he knew she would be staying a while longer. At the moment, that seemed to be all that mattered.

"I'll start the dinner," she said, turning toward the stove. "You go get your daughter."

*Your* daughter. Her very deliberately chosen words echoed in his mind as he entered Abbie's room. Abbie stood in her crib, bouncing and calling for him. "Daddy, Daddy, Daddy." He lifted her into his arms and snuggled her close, making her giggle in delight when he tickled her ribs.

*His* daughter, he thought, filled with a love for her so fierce it almost hurt. No pages from his late wife's diary, no whispered speculation, no blood tests—nothing—could ever change that.

WITH SAM'S EAGER, if untrained, assistance, Jamie prepared salad, spaghetti and garlic bread for dinner, as she had planned to do before she'd known Trevor would be there to eat it. She tried to give her full concentration to the task, but it wasn't easy, considering all the things he had said to her. She had so much to think about. And she needed time and solitude to do it.

Her thoughts kept bouncing between Trevor's admission of love and his revelations about his wife. She couldn't imagine what he must have gone through when he'd learned the truth about Melanie while still dealing with the shock of her death. To know that his acquaintances and colleagues in D.C. had already known the truth, and had been talking about it behind his back.... For a man with Trevor's pride and family history with scandal, that must have been hell.

What kind of scars would an ordeal like that leave on a man's heart and soul? And how much courage would it take to put himself at risk for anything like that again?

The questions nagged at her, making her frown and remind herself that *she* was the injured party, not Trevor. Even if she could sort of understand—at least a little—why he'd acted the way he had, that didn't mean he deserved her forgiveness. He had broken her heart. Never mind that his own must have still been shattered.

She'd always been too softhearted, she thought with a scowl. Too prone to see the other side. Too quick to forgive. Too—

"Jamie? Are you mad about something?" Sam asked.

Realizing that she had been setting the table more forcefully than necessary, she stopped thumping glasses and slamming dishes, and turned to smile at the boy. "No, Sammy, I'm not mad. I'm just in a hurry to get everything ready so we can eat. I'm hungry, aren't you?"

She wondered if she would even be able to choke down a bite.

Reassured, Sam nodded and grinned. "I'm so hungry my throat feels like my tummy's been cut."

She couldn't help laughing. "Where did you hear that?"

"From Granddad."

One of Caleb's good-old-country-lawyer expressions—which Sam had obviously turned around. Deciding not to correct him, Jamie said, "Why don't you go tell your daddy that dinner's ready?"

Trevor had been in the living room with Abbie. He

carried her into the kitchen with a smile of pride. "She's been walking for me. She took six steps without falling. She's doing great, isn't she?"

"She'll be running marathons in no time," Jamie replied without quite meeting his eyes.

"I'd better go through the house looking for hazards again. They've changed now that she's about to become more ambulatory."

Trevor put Abbie in her high chair and Jamie set a divided plastic dish holding cut-up pasta and bite-size pieces of cooked vegetables in front of her. Abbie dived in with both hands.

"Definitely have to work on table manners next," Trevor murmured.

Jamie nodded and took her seat beside Sam. Excited to have his father home again, and eager to talk about everything he'd done while Trevor had been away, Sam talked almost ceaselessly during the meal, waving his arms to emphasize his comments. Trevor had to warn him twice to calm down a bit before he spilled his drink, but other than that, he listened attentively.

Jamie tried not to stare at Trevor, but she couldn't seem to stop her eyes from turning in his direction. He was such a good father, she thought, watching him help Abbie take a sip from her cup of juice.

"This is good spaghetti, Jamie," Sam said around a mouthful.

"Don't talk with your mouth full, son."

"Thank you," Jamie told the boy, pretending not to hear Trevor's murmur. "I'm glad you like it."

Swallowing hastily, Sam added, "It's the best spaghetti I ever had."

"That's very high praise."

"I like ravioli, too. My mommy made homemade ravioli. I remember it. Do you remember, Daddy?"

Trevor never even blinked. "Your mommy cooked the best homemade ravioli in the whole world."

It touched Jamie that, despite the lingering resentment Trevor must have felt toward Melanie, he still managed to speak warmly of her to her son. And he always would, she realized. Neither Sam nor Abbie would ever hear any unpleasant word from Trevor about their mother. He would always put his own feelings aside for the sake of his children.

Everything he had done for the past year had been for the sake of his children. She wished she couldn't see that quite so clearly. It was that damn tendency of hers to see the other side again, the one that made her all too quick to understand and forgive.

Why couldn't she hold a decent grudge like other women?

"Will you come to the pool with me tomorrow and watch me swim, Daddy?" Sam continued with an artless change of subject. "Jamie said she would teach me to swim on my back. I can a little. You hold your hands like this and you swing your arms back over—uh-oh."

Quickly scooting away from the stream of spilled milk that poured out of Sam's overturned glass and dripped off the table, Jamie stood and made a grab for a paper towel.

Sam looked warily at his father. "I'm sorry, Daddy. It was an accident. I didn't mean to."

Trevor sighed lightly and moved dishes out of the way so Jamie could wipe up the spill. "I know you didn't mean to, Sam. But try to be more careful, okay?"

Relieved that he wasn't in trouble, Sam nodded firmly. "I'll be more careful. I'm sorry it dripped on your leg, Jamie."

She stood by the table, the soggy paper towel in her hand, her gaze focused on the sweet smile Trevor was giving his son. *Well, hell,* she thought in resignation. She was really going to have to work on that holding-a-grudge thing. Someday.

"That's all right, Sammy," she murmured. "Everyone makes mistakes. And everyone deserves a second chance."

Probably in response to her tone, rather than her words, Trevor's smile froze. His gaze shot to her face, narrowed, and then widened. "Jamie?"

"I forgot to make dessert," she said, her throat tightening at the almost painfully hopeful expression in his eyes. "Want to go get us some ice cream? I'll still be here when you get back."

"Ice cream?" Sam's face lit up again. "Could we have chocolate?"

"I'll, uh, go get it," Trevor muttered, but he didn't move, or look away from Jamie.

"Make mine strawberry," she told him gently, thinking that if he didn't stop looking at her that way soon she was going to burst into tears, right there in front of the kids.

"Strawberry," he repeated, sounding dazed. Still not moving.

"Daddy," Sam said impatiently, planting his little fists on his hips. "Are you going to get ice cream or not?"

Trevor suddenly grinned. "You bet I'm going to get ice cream," he said, finally coming out of his paralysis. "There's nothing I'd rather do than bring ice cream to the people I love best in the world."

Sam giggled. "Do you love Jamie?"

"Yes." His voice was low, tender.

The boy nodded matter-of-factly. "Me, too. Hurry with the ice cream, okay? My mouth's all ready for it."

Jamie laughed—and so did Trevor. It was the first time, she realized, that she had seen him really laugh. And she told herself that some rewards were definitely worth taking risks for.

"THE SUN'S COMING UP."

"That isn't the sun. It's the glow in your eyes."

Jamie looked away from the faint light coming through Trevor's bedroom window to give him a repressive look. "Don't try to be poetic, Trev, it just doesn't work for you."

He chuckled and tucked a strand of hair away from her cheek. "Sorry. I guess I'm getting a little punchdrunk. It's been a while since I've stayed up all night talking and, uh..."

She grinned. "I've particularly enjoyed the 'and, uh.'"

But the talking had been good, too, she thought,

resting her cheek on his bare shoulder. Trevor had told her more about his marriage, and the things he'd heard from his so-called friends after Melanie's funeral. It had been a horrible time for Trevor, especially after he'd found Melanie's frank, almost viciously worded journal.

Jamie had told him about her gradual realization that she hadn't been cut out for stardom, her desire to face her past, her reluctant acceptance that her parents would never be what she had always needed them to be. They had talked about dreams they'd had, mistakes they had made and the accomplishments they took pride in.

She felt as though she had shown him more of herself than anyone else had ever seen. And he'd as much as said the same when he'd admitted that he and Melanie had never really bared their souls to each other, that they had simply operated on assumptions about each other that had often proven to be wrong.

"I'd better go back to the guest room," Jamie murmured, looking again at that lightening window. "I don't want Sam to find me in here. It doesn't set a good example."

"Does this mean we have to sneak into each other's beds until after we're married?"

She lifted her head. "I don't remember anyone mentioning marriage."

"We should make it pretty soon, I think, before the gossips get started again."

"Aren't you forgetting something?"

"Like?"

"A proposal?"

Pursing his lips, he shook his head. "You might say no. Better to just forge ahead, I think."

"You've got a real sneaky side to you, did you know that, Trevvie?"

"I've asked you not to call me that."

"I'm going to call you worse if I don't get a proper proposal."

"Should I get down on one knee?"

Since they were sprawled so comfortably in his bed, she saw no need for that. "No. But I want you to say the words."

"Jamie, will you marry me?"

"Why?"

He sighed. "Why can't you ever respond the way I expect you to? It's a simple yes-or-no question."

"Why, Trev?"

"Because I love you," he said after a moment, all teasing gone. "Because I'm not stupid enough to risk losing you twice. Because I want to spend the rest of my life waiting to see what fascinating and unpredictable thing you're going to do next. Because you have so much to give to me and to my children, and I believe we have a great deal to offer you in return. I like being a part of a family. That's something I'll never take for granted again. This time, I swear I'll work at making it a success. I think I've loved you since you were a precocious teenager flirting with me behind the gym. I know I'll love you until the day I die. Is that reason enough?"

"Oh, yeah," she said shakily, swiping at her cheek with the back of one hand. "More than enough. I love you, too, Trevor McBride. And if you're sure you won't regret it, I'll marry you."

"I'll never regret it," he vowed, tugging her closer. "And I'm going to make damn sure that you never do, either."

"I never could resist a challenge," she murmured, pulling his mouth to hers.

# Epilogue

"TREVOR, you can't come in here! It's bad luck."

Trevor smiled at his sister, kissed her cheek, then firmly set her aside and stepped past her.

Dressed in a beautifully beaded white suit, Jamie stood in the center of his mother's guest room, being attended to by her other bridesmaids, Susan Schedler and his cousin Emily. Both of them frowned when they saw him.

"Too late," he said. "I've already seen her. And I can't imagine any bad luck could come from seeing my bride looking so beautiful."

Because they found that touching, the others fell silent. Jamie smiled at him. "You're trying to be poetic again," she accused him. "Okay, this time it worked."

"Could I be alone with Jamie for just a few minutes?" Trevor asked the women.

Tara planted her hands on her hips in exasperation. "Can't it wait? The wedding starts in fifteen minutes. If you're a minute late, Mother will have a hissy fit."

"We won't be late," he promised. "Not if you'll all clear out now."

Sighing and rolling their eyes, Tara, Emily and Susan left the room. "But don't blame me," Tara couldn't resist saying over her shoulder just before she closed the door, "if Mother comes in here to lead you out by your ear."

"You really do look beautiful," Trevor murmured, admiring the tiny white flowers scattered in Jamie's short red hair.

She smiled and touched his cheek. "Thank you. Now, tell me why you've barged in here. If you've gotten cold feet and decided to cancel the wedding, I swear I'll hang you in front of the guests by your toenails."

He chuckled. "You know better than that."

"Then what is it?"

He reached into the pocket of his navy suit jacket. "I wanted you to see this. It came this morning."

She took the folded sheet of paper curiously. "What is it?"

"Open it."

She did, read the dryly stated scientific facts stated upon it, then gave a little cry. "Trevor!"

His smile was shaky. "I know."

She held the paper to her heart, not caring that it was crumpling in her hands. "You're Abbie's father. This removes any doubt."

"I've always been her father," he answered firmly. "This only confirms what my heart has always known. But even if the results had been different, it wouldn't have changed anything. I would have loved her just as much."

"I know. But this really is wonderful news. She's really your daughter."

"In fifteen minutes, she'll be *our* daughter," he reminded her.

She drew a deep breath. "Oh, wow. I'm about to become a stepmom."

"There's no one I would trust more with my children," he assured her. "Or with my heart."

She dashed at her eyes. "You really have to stop this poetic thing, Trevvie. It's hell on my mascara."

Though he was smiling, he spoke in a warning growl, "If you dare call me that in front of anyone..."

Her smile turned wicked. "You know I can never resist a challenge."

He kissed her, telling her he wouldn't stop until she promised not to embarrass him in public. He was still there when his mother barged into the room to drag him out by his ear.

"I'll see you at the altar," he called over his shoulder.

"Trust me," she said. "I'll be there."

He paused just long enough to send her a smile. "As it happens, I do trust you. Implicitly."

## HARLEQUIN® Temptation.

A small town in Georgia. A family with a past. A miniseries packed with sensual secrets and elusive scandals. Bestselling author Gina Wilkins's unforgettable drama continues with...

### THE WILD McBRIDES

Be sure to watch for:

Temptation #792 **SEDUCTIVELY YOURS,**
July 2000

Temptation #796 **SECRETLY YOURS,**
August 2000

*and*

Harlequin Single Title,
**YESTERDAY'S SCANDAL,** September 2000

*Don't miss the sexy,
scandalous escapades of the McBride clan,
the most notorious family in the South!*

*Available wherever Harlequin books are sold.*

### HARLEQUIN®
*Makes any time special* ™

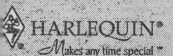
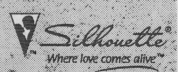

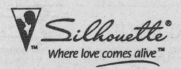

Your Romantic Books—find them at

# www.eHarlequin.com

## Visit the *Author's Alcove*

➤ Find the most complete information anywhere on your favorite author.

➤ Try your hand in the Writing Round Robin— contribute a chapter to an online book in the making.

## Enter the *Reading Room*

➤ Experience an interactive novel—help determine the fate of a story being created now by one of your favorite authors.

➤ Join one of our reading groups and discuss your favorite book.

## Drop into *Shop eHarlequin*

➤ Find the latest releases—read an excerpt or write a review for this month's Harlequin top sellers.

➤ Try out our amazing search feature—tell us your favorite theme, setting or time period and we'll find a book that's perfect for you.

All this and more available at

# www.eHarlequin.com
### on Women.com Networks

HEYRB1

# HARLEQUIN®
## Temptation.

# COMING NEXT MONTH

### #793 RULES OF ENGAGEMENT Jamie Denton

Jill Cassidy needs a fiancé—fast! Morgan Price needs a savvy lawyer—immediately! The gorgeous contractor agrees to pretend he's madly in love with her and attend her sister's wedding. In turn, Jill will settle his case. But drawing up the "rules of their engagement" brings trouble. For starters, they have to practice kissing. Then there's the single hotel room they *have* to share....

### #794 GABE Lori Foster
### The Buckhorn Brothers, Bk. 3

Gabe Kasper, the heartthrob of Buckhorn County, can have any woman he wants. But it's prickly, uptight college woman, Elizabeth Parks, who gets under his skin. She thinks Gabe's some kind of hero and wants an interview for her thesis. He doesn't consider pulling a couple of kids out of the lake heroic, but will answer her questions in exchange for kisses...and more.

### #795 ALL THROUGH THE NIGHT Kate Hoffmann
### Blaze

*Is it love...or just a one-night stand?* Advice columnist Nora Pierce can't answer that for sure. An unexpected night with warm sexy sportswriter Pete Beckett thrills her to the core. But the ex-jock is too laid back and a real ladies' man to boot. Nora can only read between the lines...and decide where to draw the line with Pete!

### #796 SECRETLY YOURS Gina Wilkins
### The Wild McBrides

Trent McBride is known for being brash, cocky and very, very reckless. But when a horrific plane crash leaves him grounded, he doesn't know what to do with his life. Then he meets spirited, *secretive* Annie Stewart and suddenly, he feels alive again. Especially when he learns that Annie desperately needs a hero....